FORGOTTEN SECRETS

FORGOTTEN SECRETS

Beverley Boissery

Wesbrook Bay Books
Vancouver, B.C.

Second Edition

Edited by Kathy Tyers
Cover Design by Katrina Johanson
Interior Book Design by BDG LeGuin

This is a revised edition of a work previously published as *The 3Js*.

Published in Vancouver, November 2018

ISBN: 978-1-928112-11-2

DEDICATION

For Lesley Bentley and Chris Greenwood

IN MEMORIAM

For William Stewart Ferguson of the Royal Winnipeg Rifles; those executed with him on the Caen-
Fountenay Road, and, for all those slaughtered in war.

1

I sat on the end of the dock, feet dangling, waiting for Mom to round the point. Up to a week ago she hadn't had any trouble. After all, she'd either rowed canoed, kayaked or paddle boarded the waters for more than thirty years. Lately, though, something was bothering her and she wasn't paying close enough attention to the tides.

We spend our summers just outside Qualicum Beach, a small town on the mainland side of Vancouver Island. Mom's family had bought several plots on what was then a deserted beach about 140 years ago when a native fisherman at the other end was the only neighbor, and she's been coming here since she was a baby. Why she's started getting stranded is a question without an answer.

Today's high tide had come and gone a couple of

hours back, so I was worried. If she got stuck, I'd have to run along the beach and help carry her board over a stretch of rocks. Easy enough job, but not one I really wanted. And so I sat, worrying, and staring at the point, oblivious even to a couple of seal pups that chased each other around the dock's pilings before racing off and returning to smack the water with their tails. They made so much noise that I didn't hear stealthy footsteps creep up behind me.

One moment I was watching the pups. The next I was in the water with them.

I knew who had pushed me. I came up spluttering and started to splash water high enough to soak him.

Mikey French laughed as he danced out of the way. "Drywall's come."

"Mom hasn't."

"She's on her way. She's fine, Jenn. Truth."

Mom verified that almost immediately. Every time she went out on her board she seemed tall and strong. Only lately, when she sat at the kitchen table did she seem to have the cares of the world on her shoulders. This was new, and it bothered me because I hadn't a clue about how I could help.

"Come on, Jenn. She'll be back by the time you shower and change. Come on. Please hurry. I really need to talk to you."

Mikey French was one of my best friends and certainly my best summer friend. His family had been on our beach longer than we had. His great-something grandfather had won the land in a poker game way when it had seemed worthless. Now Mikey and his dad summered here together with the rest of us, the Vancouver people.

By the time I changed, Mom had packed lunches for Mikey and me. She didn't have to. I was old enough to do it but fussing over me seemed one of the ways she showed love this strange summer. Mikey and I shouted our thanks, picked up our bikes and left for his house,

It used to be one of the local eyesores. Mikey's dad was a fisherman and only used the place during the summer. When we came over to QBeach for Thanksgiving, it always surprised me that their place was shut up and that Mikey was somewhere north of Campbell River with his grandparents. I suppose it was the two months or so when we were the only kids roughly the same age on the beach that had cemented our friendship years ago.

Mikey was a tiny bit taller than me, maybe five foot nine or ten. But as he was a couple of years younger, Mom thought he'd grow into a veritable giant and said, that if he lived in Vancouver, he'd have coaches drooling over him. Mikey could already throw a football as far as my twin brothers and they were going off to McGill in a couple of weeks and, when we played basketball, Mikey was the one who sank three-pointers consistently.

But the athletic paragon needed grunt help this summer and I was it. Mom had been amused and given permission, so I pulled up rotten flooring and generally made myself useful demolishing the old shack. During one of the work breaks I'd asked Mikey why his dad was doing this huge renovation.

"He's thinking of getting married. Thinks he might want to live here year round if that happens. The band got a huge new deal for some land. I got a share as well."

That was the other thing about Mikey but I don't totally understand it. I think, although his ancestor had had something to do with a European, Mikey's dad retained band membership. I frequently forgot that, although Mikey had greyish eyes, he was a First Nations or a Canadian aboriginal kid. I'd asked Mom about his grey eyes once and she told me they must have come from his French ancestor, maybe back in the 1800s. I hadn't heard about a windfall but I bet Mom could tell me about it when I got home. The key thing was that Mr. French's share was enough to turn his fishing shack into a Shaughnessy mansion.

So all summer I'd worked on making the back part of it fit for King Mikey and, with the drywall's arrival, I knew that painting would be next on my agenda. When I went home that night, I grumbled that I was nothing but unpaid labor. "What's more, Mom, he's invited himself for dinner. Is there enough? Can I do anything?"

Extra people for dinner was never a big deal for Mom. She could probably conjure up enough food for a regiment if she had to. "Does Mikey's father want to come as well? There's plenty? Tell him I could do steaks on the barbecue. Call him."

When they arrived dressed in their second best clothes, I gave a yelp and raced for my bedroom. T-shirt and shorts weren't going to cut it. But I wondered why they were being so formal. Mikey's dad would have been welcomed in his work clothes. Mikey himself, once he'd taken his jacket off, raced around the kitchen helping Mom as though he was the one who lived here. I was reduced to sitting out front, watching the seals and thinking up questions to entice Mikey's dad into conversation. He seemed more than happy to enjoy the water in silence though.

It was a happy meal. Mom had enough conversation for the four of us and, after dessert, she asked the question that bothered me. "Now," she began, "I know there's something on your mind. Why don't you tell me what it is?"

There was a long silence. I started packing up the dishes and was rather surprised when Mikey didn't help. No one said anything while I put them into the dishwasher. When I sat down I turned to Mikey. "Well, you're worried about something. Do you need our help?"

They both nodded. "It's the money, Mrs. North," Mr. French said and looked at Mom. "Even after we finish the house, there's still a huge chunk. I've upgraded the boat, it's got everything you can think of now, but I don't know what to do with Mikey's share. I've asked him, and all he'll say is school."

"School?" I was genuinely surprised. His dad had offered him a chance to fulfill his dreams and all Mikey wanted was school?

Mikey had problems at school. He didn't talk much about it – just enough so that I knew he genuinely hated it. In fact, I'd sort of worked out that he was going to have to repeat Grade 6.

"What do you mean by school, Mikey?" Mom asked in her best mother's voice.

Mikey looked over at his dad, got a nod of go-ahead, and turned to Mom. "I want to go to Dave and Dan's school. Some place where they'll actually teach me."

I read the surprise on Mom's face although she hid it well. I'd talked to her when I'd first thought Mikey might have to repeat Grade 6 because I was worried that he might say to heck with school and go fishing with his dad.

Mom was good at this though. She knew what to do, what questions to ask. "What did you mean by some place where you'd be taught?"

Mikey didn't hesitate. This wasn't the time for shyness or holding back. "I need a school where their first thought isn't that I'm a dumb Indian so it's no use spending time on me. They do, you know. Especially because Dad owns his own fishing boat. If I don't understand something, they think it's because I'm an idiot and they just leave me alone. Even when I ask for help they go all patronizing and tell me it doesn't matter if I don't know. They think because I'm Indian…"

"First Nations," my PC mother corrected.

"First Nations, aboriginal, Indian. It doesn't matter to them because they think I'm dumb and lazy. Just another Indian kid who fits their stereotype."

"They're going to make him repeat," Mikey's dad put in. "And he's the brightest kid in the school."

He had Mom's full interest. "Why do you think that?"

He didn't seem to have the words for the longest time and, while he thought, I cleared the table and made everyone decaf. "Mikey knows all about curves and things. He's the best navigator I know. It's like math is some kind of first language for him. What they try to teach him is stuff he knew before he went to school. Probably not everything," he added with a grin, "but the basics."

"They think I'm not concentrating," Mikey put in and we all heard the anger in his voice. "They don't believe me when I tell them I know it. They need to see it in a boring book. They won't even let me do the tests because I haven't done all the pretty problems first. So I'm thinking. Dave and Dan talk a lot about their math teacher, just like he's some god. I want to be in his class."

Mom gulped and to hide it served the coffee. Both she and I knew the teacher Mikey was talking about. He taught AP math.

Wow, golly gee, my sainted aunt and all the rest!

"We've looked up the St. Nicholas School for Boys on the web," Mr. French went on , "and we know we've missed all their deadlines. However, we thought if you asked, they might give Mikey a chance. He says he won't go back to do Grade 6 again, and I believe him."

I believed it as well but I also knew that St. Nick's had hundreds of boys on its waiting lists. I'd never heard of anyone deciding to come and being accepted straightaway after kindergarten. And as I listened to Mr. French talk to Mom, I learnt one other thing that made it mission impossible. He said that they'd calculated what it would cost. If Mikey had to repeat Grade 6 there, they'd need enough for seven years and Mikey's share of the money wouldn't quite cover it. He'd need a little scholarship help. A little, but some nevertheless, because he'd have to be a boarder.

St. Nick's was the best or second best school for boys in Canada. Best or second best depended on whom you talked to. Its fees were gargantuan but there seemed no limit to the number of parents who wanted to send their son there. Mikey would face international competition as well because it was one of the top targets for ambitious Chinese parents. What Mikey wanted seemed so impossible and, yet, I had this horrible feeling we absolutely had to help. What's more, I had this strange feeling that Mikey was giving St. Nick's a chance. He'd be their first and only aboriginal student doing AP math when he was old enough for sure.

Mom brought out some more wine for herself and Mikey's dad and when they began chatting, Mikey pulled me down to the water's edge. "Surprised?"

I didn't bother answering. I just threw sand at him. "Your English is pretty bad. If you go ahead with this, I'll tutor you for an hour a day."

"And you'd know enough?"

I threw more sand. "I know more than you. As long as your English is OK and your math is as good as what you say, you might be all right. But seriously, Mikey, do you know how hard it is to get into St. Nick's? Some kids go to tutors for years just to ace the interview. Worse, some boys are pretty racist."

Mikey shrugged. "Had to fight that all my life. I figure St. Nick's has to be smart enough to know the difference between genuine and tutor-taught answers."

I nodded, but I wasn't sure. I talked to Mom after they'd gone and she said I was absolutely right about getting Mikey's English up. We decided that she'd set up a series of reading and comprehension questions while I made him write a couple of paragraphs each day.

When we told him, he gave a look that made me think he hated us. Temporarily, that is.

The time spent tutoring Mikey seemed to make Mom happier somehow. She phoned St. Nick's and got an appointment to meet with Mr. Creighton, the school's headmaster. Not the Junior School's principal, but the headmaster of the whole school. I was impressed.

And therefore unprepared for what I heard when I came back for lunch from Mikey's just before summer's end. When I opened the door and walked towards the kitchen, I heard Mom explode at someone, "What do you mean it's impossible?"

I couldn't hear any answer so I figured Mom had to be on the phone. For a horrible moment I wondered if it were St. Nick's, telling Mom they wouldn't even go to the trouble of interviewing Mikey, but my diplomatic Mom would have been far more controlled. So I waited while whoever-it-was defended the impossibility of whatever-it-was and was astonished to hear real anger in Mom's voice when she said, "I simply cannot accept that."

I thought about sneaking into the kitchen and grabbing something out of the fridge. Mom never – well, maybe once or twice – lost her temper. She sat at the breakfast bar, tapping a pencil on the counter, while she stared at her calendar. I must have made some noise because she pointed to the fridge and then looked back at her calendar.

"I simply will not accept it, Jonathan," she said in a very quiet voice, going from volcano to iceberg in those seven words. I edged closer to check out her calendar and suddenly understood. Mom had planned her twenty-fifth wedding anniversary for months. She'd investigated every possible site in cyber-verse before deciding that she and Dad would go to Bora-Bora in Tahiti. Dad had agreed and they'd marked off three weeks in March. Of course, *sans moi*. But Dad must have discovered a conflict with that date and knowing him, it would be work-related. Law firm first, anniversary second.

Mom must have understood that as well. She sounded weary when she said, "Well, that's fine, Jonathan. If you can't come, you can't. But I am not cancelling the arrangements. I'll go by myself." She jabbed down on the end-call button but didn't say anything. She just sat and stared at her calendar. I put two placemats on the table, made a salad, put a cold lunch together and poured some ice tea. She didn't seem to notice, even though I rushed out to the garden for a couple of sprigs of fresh mint. Finally she came across to the table and thanked me. She didn't seem to eat anything, although she pushed food around her plate like a toddler. She just sat there with a peculiar look on her face and I felt useless because I couldn't think of anything to say to make her feel better.

It was a horrible meal and only when I put our few plates into the dishwasher did things start to get better. The gate to the street opened amid the sound of turbulence. The twins had arrived. Unless you knew her well, you would not have known anything was wrong with Mom though. She hugged the twins, asked what they had planned, and acted like everything was normal.

Dan took one look at her and said, "Mom, I've got something especially for you in the car. Come and help me in with it."

I suppose it says everything that Mom didn't seem to suspect that he was manipulating the truth. As soon as she started out towards their car, Dave jerked his thumb towards the beach and as soon as we reached it said, "Come on, little sister. What's up?"

"Dad quit on Tahiti. Mom's just found out."

Dave said a few words that he didn't usually say in front of me then asked, "What can we do?"

I shrugged. I didn't have a clue. "We ate out last night, but if you go down to the wharf and buy some

Dungeness crabs, I'll make supper and give you lots of time to visit with her. Just talk happy stuff. Like your idiot idea for making the soccer team or something. Tell her why you're doing different sports."

The twins always played on the same team whatever sport they did. However they knew their chances of both making one of McGill's teams were tough, so Dave decided he'd try out as a goalie in soccer while Dan took his chances with the basketball teams. Dave stared at the water for several moments before saying, "I'll give it my best shot. Maybe we'll stay in tonight and talk then."

Their week at Qualicum had been planned as something like a rock band's farewell tour with parties every night. The mere fact that Dave was willing to stay home should have told me that monsters lurked ahead but like, the captains of old, I ignored the warning. But Mom brushed them off and in the end they went out as they'd planned.

She was quiet after they left and, although my meal should have had three stars from Michelin, she didn't seem to notice. She and I sat outside on our Adirondack chairs with neither of us saying anything. An Alaska cruise ship glided by across from us on the other side of the strait and I imagined the passengers' excitement over their first night on board. Some must have been fussing over their clothes for dinner, others making new friends with pre-dinner drinks in the bar. Maybe a few wished they'd stayed home.

I wished I was there. That's the thing about Qualicum Beach. It's on Vancouver Island, on the side that faces the mainland. It's not terribly touristy. Mom says she did the same things as I usually do — except renovating Mikey's house of course. She means going out on the water. In her day it was rowboats and canoes. I boogie-board, paddle board and kayak. We sit out at night just like she did with her mom. Occasionally a salmon plops in the water, the seals hunt their meals and people walk by on the beach with their dogs. Watching this, just vegetating *is* wonderful and something I miss when we're back in Vancouver. My Vancouver friends don't like it though.

Amalie and Emilie Zhou came the last two summers and were totally bored. Qualicum Beach doesn't have malls. There was nothing else that they liked to do, so they did nothing but complain. I don't know if they would have done the same this summer or if I'd have even asked them to come but their dad got transferred to New York so I didn't have the problem. I imagine they're happily roaming around

Fifth Avenue now and debating Louis Vuitton versus Gucci.

I don't ever think of QBeach as a vacation, although it sometimes takes five hours to get there from Vancouver. It's sort of like an extension of home. The sheets and towels are the same, although my bed is the original cedar bunk. We drive in the same car, eat much the same food with the major difference being that the salmon and crabs are always caught a few hours before we eat them. It's marvelous but it's not like going someplace and nothing like Mom what will do when she goes to Bora-Bora.

The twins always call me a spoilt brat when I get like this and I guess I am. But maybe because I've never known any other kind of summer and because I've been coming here since I was born, really does mean that I can't appreciate QBeach properly. One of the scholarship girls at school went to Disney World last summer and she talked about it the whole year. Mom will never take me to Disney World because she thinks it's "common." That means, I think, everyone can go to Disney World, if their save their money, but only we can come to our place on the beach.

Sometimes, like tonight though, I think I'd like common.

Anyway, Mom and I sat in silence. I tried to imagine what she was thinking about. We were used to Dad letting us down. Bailing on his twenty-fifth anniversary though seemed unthinkable. Especially because he'd promised Mom in front of all of us that he wouldn't let work interfere with it. Mom had paid for the flights and hotels a couple of months ago and every now and then I'd catch her checking out her Bora-Bora hut on her computer.

Tahiti meant a lot to Mom and I was glad she had stood her ground. She'd got as used to Dad not showing up for things as much as we had, but this time she'd told him she didn't care what he did, she was going anyway. And then as I went over their conversation, I realized something. Something huge. She hadn't cancelled the arrangements. That meant there were still *two* first class seats booked, *two* places at the resort, and *only* Mom going.

Another cruise ship went by and this time I was totally uninterested. My mind whirled with dreams. Eventually, I got my courage together. I reached across and touched Mom's arm. "You know I overheard you and Dad, don't you?"

Her lips tightened into a straight line and for a moment I thought she'd cry. Then she nodded.

"Well," I ploughed on, "can I go with you?"

I said it as straight out as that. No brilliant lead-up. No flattery. Just that one question.

Mom didn't answer. We must have sat in total silence for five minutes. At first I wondered if she was working out how to make the changes. After all, Dad's passport number was attached to one of the tickets and there must have been other obstacles I didn't know about. Then I thought the ideas must have been so repugnant that they weren't worth an answer. When I'd given up hope, she turned to me, "It's in school time."

"But Grade 9 school time. Nothing happens in Grade 9. I could easily miss three weeks. Four, even."

Quiet again. I sat back and felt hopeful. She hadn't turned the idea down. Then she astonished me by saying, "You know, Jenn. You're getting to be good company."

I sat in a pleased silence. I didn't know what to say and then Mom's hand touched my cheek, like she used to when I was a little kid. "Straight As, Jenn. And ninety-five in English and Social Studies. At the very least."

My hands clenched into fists of happiness. Ours wasn't a particularly demonstrative family. I don't know why. Maybe Mom thought hugs were "common." But that touch and her words were as good as any hug. After a while I went upstairs and thought about what she had said. I knew ninety-four wouldn't cut it. I had to get a grade of ninety-five in English and Social Studies. Of course, kind Mrs. Robertson would be teaching me and I knew I could plead for the extra percent or two if I needed it.

Especially if I told her I had started reading the books during the summer. That meant that I'd beg Dave or Dan to drive into the village and buy the two first term books – Shakespeare's *A Midsummer Night's Dream* and *The Diary of Anne Frank*. If I got those read, I could concentrate on Mrs. Robinson's assignments.

That night I dreamed of Bora-Bora.

2

Next morning Mom threw her energy into getting Mikey ready for St. Nick's, deciding to add public speaking to the things he had to know. And now I found to my dismay, her lessons included me. Sometimes she'd give us a topic that we had to prepare four minute speeches on. At other times, she'd point something out, like a cruise ship, and say, "Jenn, in thirty seconds I want a two minutes talk about that ship."

At first it spooked us. Mikey began wondering if his dream of St. Nick's was worth all the "speechifying." But after a while we buckled down because we could see the benefits. Mikey now stood tall when he began speaking and he always looked at us. After a while he could talk (not always sensibly though) on anything. One night the twins were there and Dave told Mikey he wanted to hear two minutes about McGill University.

Mikey glared but then stood, swallowed and began, "McGill is an old university In Montreal, Quebec. In September it will include two students from British Columbia who have many bright ideas, mostly about breaking rules around alcohol. For example, I remember how they managed to buy beer when they were only fourteen…"

When Mom looked extremely interested, Dan threw a cushion and told Mikey to shut up. Mikey's smile was pure smug.

As for me, I knew Mrs. Robinson loved public speaking. Now I began to work out that Mom was pulling for me. She wanted me in Tahiti with her and all this work would guarantee me a better grade in English. I guess people show love in different ways. Mom might not hug but she was making sure that when I got up to speak with people I would be as polished and assured as possible. She was doing everything to help me get that A in public speaking.

Summer had almost finished when I realized that Dad hadn't come over much. Usually he flew in on the late flight on Thursday or Friday nights and went back to Vancouver on Sunday. Every now and then I heard Mom arguing with him on her phone. She had hardly ever argued with him until he'd broken his promise about Tahiti.

With only five days left at QBeach, I felt proud of myself. I'd helped renovate a house, pounded nails and acquired painting skills. I'd worked hard to beat the twins in paddle-boat races and been an asset on their pick-up basketball games. On a different level I felt confident about Grade 9. I'd tracked down and read both the key English books and had even memorized little bits of Shakespeare. Mom told me I now looked comfortable when I gave my talks and speeches so, all in all, I thought my ninety-five per-cent in English was pretty-much guaranteed.

Then Dad phoned and said he was coming over on the last weekend for a family conference. Dave and Dan argued because they had planned to fly out to Montreal that Friday morning. The fact that Dad had changed their flight to Sunday afternoon and upgraded them to business class took only a tiny bit off their anger.

"He's had all summer for a family pow-wow," Dan fumed. "All summer. Now we get in at midnight on Sunday and start classes on Tuesday. We won't know where to go or how to get there."

That was silly. They knew. They been working out metro routes with the same intensity that Mom had used when narrowing down which Tahiti resort she wanted to stay at. I didn't care. If I didn't see Dad on the weekend, I'd see him the following day when we went home. It seemed a tempest in a teapot.

He arrived as scheduled Friday night with two briefcases, a permanent frown and none of us were surprised when he headed for his office after supper. I sleep above Mom and Dad's bedroom and until I eventually dozed off, I heard them arguing. Dave and Dan took me out in their boat the next day. I suppose they felt as miserable as I did because they certainly looked worried. They should have been in Montreal.

That night, after the twins and I put the dishes into the dishwasher, Dad started the conference. He was moving to Toronto on Tuesday to become managing partner of the family law firm, North & Pickering, LLP.

To some extent this made sense. Mom's family was old — in Vancouver terms. Dad's family dated back to the founding of Toronto, one hundred years before Vancouver even existed. One of my North ancestors, a great-great-great something or other, had founded the family's law firm in the 1840s and the eldest son had always been managing partner. But Dad had given that up when he married Mom, a west coast girl. Uncle Gerald had leapt at the chance to be boss-in-chief. Dad had built up a Vancouver branch of the firm and everyone had been happy.

One of the twins asked the obvious. "Why? What's changed?"

"Uncle Gerald has cancer. It's terminal." We sat in stunned silence and Dad broke it to go on, "I've got no other choice. I owe it to the family."

This time the stunned silence was longer. "Oh, I see," Dan said eventually. "It's the family that counts. Not us."

A vein started pulsing in Dad's forehead. It looked gross but I couldn't stop staring at it. I think it helped dull the anger in Dad's words. "You don't understand. You've been sheltered out here. The firm needs a North at its masthead if we're to avoid being gobbled up by an international conglomerate. We're independent and we want to stay that way."

I studied my placemat and wondered what schools in Toronto were like. That is, until I looked at Mom's face. It was tight. Expressionless. Closed off. She showed no emotion until Dad said she was going to give living in eastern Canada a try.

"Tell them the truth, Jonathan," she exploded, all passivity gone. "Tell them it's not living in Toronto that's on trial. It's our marriage." She looked at the twins and me and I wondered why I had ever thought

Mom unemotional. "Your father," she went on, "has put his very persuasive skills to work. I *was* planning on getting a divorce. Now I've agreed to hold off until December."

A divorce? In *our* family. Mom and Dad had always seen divorce as a sign of failure and I'd pitied the girls who had single parent families. Now it looked like I was months away from being one of them. I didn't realize I was crying until Mom reached across and dried the tears on my cheeks with her hand. "This is going to hit you the hardest, Jenn," she said gently.

"In so many ways," Dad added." I've missed you this summer. You've grown a foot and you're becoming a beautiful young lady. I know I'm going to miss you when I go to Toronto."

His words didn't make sense. He'd miss me when he went to Toronto? I felt like the world had gone topsy-turvy. Nothing made sense. I stopping crying and turned to Mom, "Won't we live with Dad in Toronto?"

She beckoned to me. "Come and sit." I hadn't sat in Mom's lap for years. I couldn't remember when and I think Mom realized that I was as tall as she was because she stood and pointed to the living room. "Let's adjourn. Jenn, sit by me and we'll explain."

We waited while Dad got himself a drink and then

the twins grabbed a beer. I grabbed hold of Mom. She suddenly seemed the only solid thing in my universe. Dad started talking on his way in, "It doesn't make any sense to uproot you seeing that your mother seems hell-bent on this divorce."

The twins had hidden most of their anger but now it surfaced and I thought Dave was going to punch Dad out. "Are you saying that you're leaving Jenn all by herself in Vancouver while you swan off to Toronto? Because if you are, Dan and I will go to UBC."

Dad shook a dismissive hand. "Don't jump to conclusions. No, Jenn will be all right. She'll keep going to Primrose Heights but she'll become a boarder."

I felt my head spin again and I'm sure my mouth dropped open. It was too many shocks at once. Every morning of my entire school life I'd been dropped off at Prim Heights and either been picked up in the afternoon or I'd taken the bus home. Dad might think everything was "all right" but it wasn't. While the Junior School was on the same campus as the Senior School, the boarding houses were on a nearby street and their inmates walked to and from school. What's more there was something of a war between them and us, the regular day students. They thought they were the elite. We knew they weren't. Now, Dad thought I'd be okay? He didn't understand that it felt like I'd just become a prisoner of war.

Mom came upstairs with me when I went to bed and hugged me until I cried myself to sleep.

* * * * *

When your universe shatters and it doesn't seem possible that things can get any worse, you block out the terrifying things. Then, it's the small irritants that jump in and grab you.

I couldn't bear to think of Mom and Dad in Toronto, the twins in Montreal, and me thousands of kilometres away from them all. I hated Mom and Dad's bitter war. I couldn't even work out whether or not I wanted them to stay together.

So instead, I went ballistic over the school's uniforms. Not uniforms *per se*. I'd always worn one to school. But if I were a boarder, I had to get new clothes. Like just about every other girls' school in Vancouver, we wore plaid kilts. The day skirt was a pattern of light brown squares offset by smaller checked squares of powder blue, royal blue and dark brown. The boarders' dominant color was powder blue and they wore powder blue fleeces instead of brown. I knew it didn't make sense, but when the universe goes out of kilter, you obsess on the irrelevant.

I quickly found out, as well, that getting ready for boarding was hard work. There was a list of things we had to check off: ten pairs of underwear, two swimsuits and three towels, and enough clothes to get me from fall to winter. Then there were raincoats, winter coats, umbrellas, hats, gym stuff and the going out for dinner clothes. You name it — it was on the list.

It took three long days to get everything together. As I tried to help Mom with her own chores, I could not have felt more miserable. Not only was I going back as a boarder; I would now be two days late. The best lockers would be taken and everyone would know the latest gossip, including why I had to board. There were few secrets at Prim Heights.

To make matters worse, Mr. French phoned. Mikey had broken his leg and wouldn't be able to come across for his St. Nick's interview. Could Mom reschedule it? Mom phoned, did her best, and her best resulted in another chance for Mikey, but it was after she left for Toronto.

"What will he do?" I asked and wondered when the calamities would end.

"You'll have to go with him. You can take my

place and be his 'parent'. Mr. Creighton's okayed it. I'll arrange for him to be picked up at the ferry and you can take a taxi over to St. Nick's and meet him there."

"What will I say?" I said, and I know I sounded hysterical. I'd vaguely thought of becoming a parent in twelve to fifteen years and I'd certainly hadn't imagined my first child would be taller than me. But when I calmed down and looked at it logically, Mikey's chances had always been non-existent. Now they had become an absolute zero.

Time raced by. The dreaded new uniforms arrived and Mom thought I looked better in them than in the regular ones. When she finally loaded everything up and took me to Leith House, my temporary home, I had become reconciled to four months of hell. Mrs. Sinclair, the house mother, apologized to Mom. Everyone had been assigned rooms before she got the news about me. An extra bed might fit in one of the dorms but she suggested I might like to take the single attic room that they kept for emergencies instead. That way nobody would be disturbed.

It sounded fine. I didn't care if I socialized or not. So before Mom could say anything, I jumped in. "I'll take it, Mrs. Sinclair. Thank you."

She and Mom helped me get most of my belongings up the stairs. While I unpacked, Mrs. Sinclair explained boarder rules to me. Getting permission to go shopping was relatively easy—only, I'd have to have a senior girl willing to go with me. Going to the little shops nearby needed something called a "village privilege," and it was only given occasionally.

Like a Grade 12 would really want to go shopping with a Grade 9? Village privileges?

If I wanted to go to a friend's place on the weekend or out for Friday dinner, I needed Mom's written permission. While we had to be in uniform to eat breakfast, we could change into "smart casual," whatever that meant, for dinner and weekend meals. Homework was scheduled between 6:30 to 8:30 each night, and exemptions from it were few and far between. There was a precious hour of free time after homework, but we had in bed with lights off at 9:45.

I wasn't a Prim Heights student anymore. I was the latest grunt in the marines.

I didn't say anything as I felt life and liberty being crushed and taken away. I didn't even look at Mom. She was staying around till Monday morning, so she arranged right there and then to spring me out for the weekend.

By the time Mrs. Sinclair wound down, I had done most of my unpacking. All I had to do was give my teeth and hair another brush, put my brand new powder blue fleece on and walk down to the school with Mom. Then I'd face the first day paperwork and catch up on the school news.

Last June, there had been word of a new elective—junior creative writing. When I'd made up my schedule, I'd left a space for it. Now, as more of a protest than anything, I signed up for Competitive Sports instead. The twins had turned me into a respectable basketball player over the summer and, according to my coach last year, I was an excellent volleyball setter. Comp Sports meant that I'd play after school and on weekends. Mom had never allowed this because it interfered with our social life. But with my social life suddenly restricted to Leith House, Comp Sports sounded great. More than great, actually. Pounding the air out of balls seemed a great way to release the wall of hostility inside me.

By the end of the day, I felt that if I had to endure like one more sympathetic smile or one more "I'm sorry," I'd become absolutely insane. I did not want to be pitied. What I wanted was a friend to tell the whole gory mess to. But, with Emilie and Amalie Zhou in New York, I didn't have a single best friend left. Lots of friends, but nobody to share with.

By two o'clock I was telling myself, one more class. Just one more class. I could get through this. I could zone through English and then race back to the safety of my attic in Leith.

I should have read the school news in my first day package more carefully. Mrs. Robinson had taken a sabbatical. A new teacher, Dr. Collins, now taught Grade 9 English and Socials only she had changed its name to Humanities 9. I hated Dr. Collins on sight. She made me stand up when she introduced herself to me. Then she told me that twenty years ago she'd sat in the exact same desk as I was in for her English classes with Mrs. Robinson. Her laugh sounded like a hyena's and she showed teeth when she talked about the hand-me-down tradition of Anne Frank assignments. Things, she promised, would be different this year.

No Anne Frank assignment when I'd just spent the summer reading the book?

I slouched back in the "exact same desk," my hands fisted deep in the pockets of my new fleece and glared at her, thinking that with everything else in my life upside down, I should have expected English to change as well.

Dr. Collins ignored my glare and went on to outline our year. The Shakespeare play would be *Romeo and Juliet*. That didn't sound so bad, although I wondered if it might be boring. After all, everyone knows the "Romeo, Romeo, wherefore" line from it. As well, Dr. Collins thought it might be "nice" to concentrate on B.C. poets. One of them, Diane Tucker, would come next week to give a reading. In addition, although we would still read Anne Frank's diary, it was to be teamed with another novel, *Pied Piper,* written by an author I'd never heard of—Nevil Shute. Dr. Collins said it was about an old man leading a bunch of refugee children out of Nazi-occupied France. That would be her theme for our year in Humanities 9—the effects of war on families and refugees. Very politically correct.

And *then* she segued into the big assignment. She was keeping Mrs. Robinson's tradition of giving it seventy percent but she wanted a lot for that seventy percent — an oral presentation backed up by a written report full of documentation. She handed out a sheet with twenty suggested projects, all related to her theme. During the rest of class, we had to think about her suggestions and rank the three we'd like most to work on.

I felt so grateful to Mom for her public speaking lessons. The oral presentation would be a breeze and I read the list carefully with Tahiti in mind. There didn't seem to be anything that I could use my knowledge of Anne Frank on so I kept scanning, looking for something easy that would give me the ninety-five percent Mom expected.

Finally, I found it.

Topic 17 asked us to research an ancestor's life during World War II. We were supposed to interview any surviving relatives, and above all, find "primary sources"—something tangible from the 1940s, like a photocopy of an old newspaper. I wanted to scream and shout. Finally the string of calamities had stopped. This was my dream topic.

You see, I'm Jennifer Anne North, daughter of Jennifer Anne Morton, granddaughter of Jennifer Anne Lascelles. My great-great-great grandmother was Jennifer Anne Fraser, one of the first girls to go to Primrose Heights in 1885. Vancouver wasn't even a city then and Primose Heights was its only school.

I checked off 17 on Dr. Collin's paper and gloated. One of my great-aunts must have been at Prim Heights during World War II. What's more, I knew Mom had a stack of historical stuff somewhere and I could use it and the school's library for my "primary sources." It was ideal. Easy, easy, easy.

But then Dr. Collins dropped the "kick-you" part, the last straw that made me really hate her. After she'd collected our wish lists, she explained that if everyone worked more cooperatively, there'd be fewer wars. Therefore she'd assign us into groups of three or four. The projects would be collaborative efforts and she guaranteed that we'd get one of our three choices. As I'd only written down number 17, that didn't help me.

I despise, abhor and abominate group projects.

From my experience there's always a floater, someone who never does her share of work. Last year, Cathy Semple added herself to a group I was in and did absolutely nothing but complain. Amelie, Jeannette and I had done all the work, but she got the exact same mark as we did. It hadn't been fair. But when I thought of the family project, I relaxed. It would take work, but work that had to be done individually. Even if I did get stuck with Cathy again, she couldn't expect me to interview her grandparents, could she?

For some reason, and I don't know why, I suddenly trusted that Dr. Collins would make sure none of us floated. Furthermore, I thought I saw a twinkle in her eye when she promised to read each and every report and not be impressed by any bling, like a contest for an iPad. The top mark last year had gone to Emily Zhou and her iPhone prize.

But that new found trust went the way of the dodo bird when she told us who we'd be working with. She called my group the 3Js because I'd be with a new girl from Australia called Joelle Carstairs and Jaslyn Green a girl I dislike more than anyone in the entire school, except Dr. Collins maybe.

That's because she got me kicked out of the youth group at church last year. You'd think it would be impossible to get kicked out of church youth group but it happened. I don't drink or swear or, horror of horrors, have sex with anyone. Not yet, anyway. But I missed a crucial Bible Study class. The Zhous had asked me to go skiing with them that particular weekend and Mom had okayed it. But when it came to explaining that I wouldn't be able to go to Bible Study because I was going skiing, I jammed and told the leader I was sick. Then I'd gone to Whistler. Jaslyn had found out somehow and made sure everyone knew I'd lied. I could have apologized but staying away was much easier.

I don't understand Jaslyn. She's smart and at Prim Heights on full scholarship. She's the one who went to Disney World. But the church thing? When we go to church, we walk. Jaslyn's mother drives clear across town every Sunday to go to our church. Mom says it's for the preaching. I don't know. I don't go to adult church much but I haven't heard a sermon worth driving from one end of Vancouver to the next to listen to.

But if Jaslyn Green was bad karma, Jo Carstairs was God's gift.

Her dad was a Canadian ambassador so she'd lived in Australia the last ten years. After he'd been posted back to Canada, he'd let Jo pick what school she wanted to go to. She'd have to board because he'd be in Ottawa until January. Then he'd take early retirement and come to Vancouver. Jo's Australian school had been in a place called Rose Bay, so she said she had chosen Primrose Heights because of the rose part of our name. I'd bet she Googled us though. I would have. Just to make sure.

Jo's hot. If she were twenty pounds lighter, she could be a top model. Like me she's blond, but her hair has the kind of golden streaks in it that Mom pays gazillion bucks for. She's tall, as well. I'm five feet eight but Jo must be a good five or six inches taller. When we have our first dance with St. Nick's, the basketball guys will stand in pools of drool.

Jo's also the most genuinely nice person I've ever met. Last night when she found out that I had the attic room, she banged on my door. She'd organized her roommates, spoken to Mrs. Sinclair, and arranged for an extra bed to go into her dorm. "No one should be by themselves. Not when we can have fun together," she announced, sounding as if she, not me, had been at Prim Heights all her life.

I thought about my quiet, private room for all of three seconds. Somehow I knew that if I didn't take this chance, I'd lose myself in misery and loneliness for the rest of the year. I already felt like my family had abandoned me. What if I didn't take this chance to get a faux-family?

Seeing that Jo had bothered to go out of her way for me, I decided to do the same. Ordinarily, it would have been easy. I'd simply ask if she wanted to come home with me for the weekend but now I only had one chance to do it. On the way to school I called Mom, told her about Jo and asked, "Can you work it so she can come tonight?"

"I'm so glad you've found a friend," Mom began in that putting-off voice that told me her brain was working. "But you're not giving me much time, Jenn."

"If you phone Jo's dad, he could fax permission. I've got his private cell number." Then I let a little wheedling tone creep into my voice, "You're glad we've made friends. I bet he'll be the same."

Silence. Mom was thinking. "I'll try," she said

eventually. "Now, about tonight. I'm busy downtown all afternoon tying up loose ends. What time are you free?"

"We've got volleyball till five."

"Perfect. Take a taxi, drop your packs at the house, and meet me in the lobby of the Pan Pacific. Wear good clothes and bring swimsuits, Jenn."

Great, I thought. Mom's going to take us out for dinner. The swimsuits puzzled me. I don't know of a single underwater restaurant in Vancouver but there could one in this new topsy-turvy world of mine.

Mom must have been super-persuasive on the phone to Mr. Carstairs because, when we went to lunch, Mrs. Sinclair beamed when she told Jo she could go home with me. "It's nice to see you two making friends."

Like Jo was hard to be friends with!

I was excited, though. This was going to be a great weekend and my last good one for a while. Even the sight of Jaslyn Green back at school didn't wipe the smile from my face. It did make me realize that Jo and I would be playing in tournaments most weekends, so the three of us really needed to get together to work out a plan for Dr. Collins's project. Still smiling, I walked across to Jaslyn.

"Have you thought about the assignment yet?"

She had a shuttered look on her face, one which almost said she didn't want to see me. "Not much," she muttered.

"Well, here's what I'm thinking. Jo's coming home with me this weekend. It's my last one with Mom," I began and then stopped because Jaslyn's face got this really queer look on it. A like-she-knew-something-that-I-didn't-know-and-wouldn't-like-if-I-did kind of look.

"Um," I stumbled on, "why don't you come over to my house Sunday afternoon? You can get to know Jo a bit and we can talk about stuff. What do you think? Is Sunday afternoon okay?"

"I'll be there," she said with that strange look on her face again. "After church. Sunday."

I said good-bye and almost flounced away. After all, I was just trying to be kind and get us organized. I was sacrificing precious time with Mom and all she could do was give me that funny look and no thanks for organizing this. "Some people," I said to Jo.

"Give her time. She's afraid of you."

I frowned. I disliked Jaslyn, but she didn't have anything to be afraid of. I hadn't killed her after the Bible Study episode, had I? Jo changed the subject, and we started to think of things to do on Saturday if Mom didn't have special plans for us.

Turned out that Mom did. Have plans, that is, as we found out on Friday night. She'd booked us into the Pan Pacific's spa. Neither of us had ever gone to one before so it was a luxury I could get used to. We were oiled and massaged, had manicures and pedicures and afterwards we swam in the hotel's heated outdoor saltwater pool. Then Mom took us to the restaurant, a movie and finally home.

The next day we did touristy things to show Jo what Vancouver was all about. Like the Grouse Grind, a monstrous climb straight up Grouse Mountain. We drove through Stanley Park and afterwards rode the little ferries that buzz around False Creek and Granville Island.

As we were coming home, it hit me. I had a million things to ask Mom yet I didn't have a minute. Somehow she had put everything together, all this stuff, and when we could have talked, like late at night, I was too tired to do anything but sleep. It was funny. Almost like Mom was avoiding me by making us have fun. Tomorrow, I told myself. Tomorrow, before church. We'll talk then.

But Mom looked really nervous about something the next morning and I wondered if it was about Toronto. After all, she'd be seeing a lot of my grandmother. Mom and I call her Attila-ess, the Huness. Or maybe Mom had decided to go ahead on the divorce and was only working out how to tell everyone, particularly Attilla-ess. Anyway, she looked jumpy after church and, impossibly, jumpier as we walked home.

I'd just closed the front door, when I saw Mrs. Green's car pull up outside. I frowned. Jaslyn was supposed to come after lunch—not for it.

3

We walked to the door together. I didn't know what to do, whether to invite them in for lunch or not but Mom rescued me. "Come on in," she said, "lunch is almost ready."

Lunch? Mom had asked Mrs. Green for lunch? Why hadn't she told me? Didn't she understand the way I felt about Jaslyn? Mom had carved good manners into me though so I meekly swallowed my anger along with my questions.

As Mom ladled out the soup, her hands shook a couple of times. It was great soup, ginger pumpkin, one of my favourites, and the fresh bread for the make-your-own sandwiches had cheese and olives in it. Obviously Mrs. Green must have brought it, because we hadn't been to a bakery. Mom and Mrs.

Green had a glass of white wine in front of them, and there was sparkling water for us.

This luncheon had been planned carefully but you could have cut the tension in the room with a knife.

I wasn't surprised when Mom cleared her throat, but what she said angered me beyond reason. She welcomed the Greens, mother and daughter to the house and hoped they'd enjoy it. Then, with a smile as fake as any celebrity, she explained that Mrs. Green would be our live-in housekeeper-caretaker while the family was in Toronto. "It's brilliant, Jenn," she went on, "you'll be able to come here on weekends."

For two or three seconds I stared at the eyes and skin of an alien. No way this was my mother. Didn't she understand how I'd feel when I imagined Jaslyn sleeping in my room and pawing through my stuff? I tossed my napkin on to the table, pushed the chair back, raced upstairs to my room and stuffed everything into my backpack. Didn't she know that I felt I had no control over my life right now and that, for the first time in my life, I felt that school was better than home?

Mom stopped me at the door. "Jenn," she said, and there was a world of pleading in her voice.

I pushed past her. She grabbed my arm and forced me to look back at her. "What hurts the most?"

I didn't know. It wasn't really Mrs. Green or Jaslyn being in the house. But the Greens had been one surprise too many. "Living," was all I could say.

"Oh, Jenn," Mom said and hugged me. I stood as still as the proverbial statue. Hugs didn't cut it anymore. "Jenn," Mom went on, and her voice sounded like I'd hurt her, "Mrs. Green is the perfect choice for looking after the house. We both know her and she needs the money. I thought it would be easier for you if you knew you could always come here for weekends."

"I'd rather go to Toronto," I told her and I winced inside when I heard the disdain in my voice.

Mom didn't get it. "Jenn," she said, "it's only until Christmas. Maybe. By then I'll either be back here or you can transfer to Bishop Strachan or some other school back east."

Satan would become an ice dancer before I'd go to Bishop Strachan and walk around with the silly sailor's collar on their uniform's shirt. We'd had a substitute teacher once who thought Bishop Strachan the best girls school. In the world. Period. Every single girl in our class hated it and eventually someone in the back of the room called out that we'd puke if she mentioned BS again.

Mom and I were talking to each other through

concrete walls. It was useless. I extricated myself from her arms. "Mom, I want to go back to Leith. Can you drive me or should I get a taxi?"

Not only had I hurt Mom now but I'd managed to outrage her. "Jennifer Anne North," she told me, "you have guests in the house. They don't deserve this."

Neither did I. But Mom was right. Jo, at least, certainly didn't deserve it. Jaslyn, I couldn't bear to think about. Our World War II group had just become the group from hell. For a moment, as I started to trudge downstairs, I thought about Cathy Semple. At least she didn't intrude. She was too lazy to do that. Maybe Dr. Collins would allow us to trade her for Jaslyn.

That hope faded as soon as I saw Jaslyn and Jo in the den, chatting away like they'd known each other forever. They ignored my red eyes and suggested we get to work. "After all," Jo said, "two of us have to get back to school in time for chapel."

I'd forgotten that. Sunday night chapel was a boarder thing. In a way it was like a curfew, and we had to get back in time for it. In another way it was a hangover from Prim Heights's beginnings as an Anglican school. As a day girl it was easy to forget that, because much of the Anglican tradition had eroded with time.

I will owe Jo Carstairs till my dying day for the way she made everything easier that afternoon. I had planned to sort of chair the meeting, but she took charge and somehow made it like we were three friends talking.

"We've got to get ourselves organized," she began. "I asked Dr. Collins what she meant by backing everything up with primary documents, and she told me that she expected Xerox copies of coupon books, military records, movie tickets, newspapers from the 1940s. She said anything that would show us what it was like to live then was fine."

"I can't begin to imagine it," Jaslyn said rather timidly, looking at me as if she expected me to hit her or something.

"Nor can I," I contributed, more to make her feel at ease than anything else. She was as innocent in this mess as I was. She couldn't help what our mothers had cooked up.

At this first sign of emotion, Jo intervened. "Well, first of all, we've got to work out which rellie we're going to study."

"Rellie?" Jaslyn asked.

"Australian slang for relative," she explained with a laugh, before turning serious again. "I want to work on finding out about my great-grandfather. Dad said he was something of a hero. All I know for sure is that he died on D-Day."

Immediately I thought of blood-soaked beaches. Movies had made D-Day so familiar that it was hard to think of the soldiers as real people. Same with great-grandfathers. They'd lived so long ago.

In a way, that was good. Five years ago Jo's mom had been killed in a pedestrian crossing. Researching her great-grandfather wouldn't be like Jo researching her mom's death and trying to find the hit-and-run driver who'd killed her. That would have been tough.

"What about you Jenn? Who's your target?"

I felt ashamed. I'd chosen a female "rellie" because I thought it would be easy. "Nobody as heroic as your great-grandfather," I said with a slight shrug. "I thought I'd try my great-grandmother or a great-aunt. All the females in Mom's family have gone to Prim Heights, so finding primary sources won't be hard. I don't know who it is exactly yet. I have to ask Mom."

"Better hurry," Jo commented. "She leaves tomorrow, doesn't she?"

I nodded as my fear and anger returned. "Doesn't matter, does it? Now I know that I can get into the house on weekends, all Mom has to do is tell me where the old papers and stuff are stored." I was back into my glooming at the thought. To break out of it, I turned to Jaslyn. "Who have you picked, Jaslyn?"

Her head went down so that we couldn't see her face. "I don't know," she said so softly that we had to strain to hear. "I don't know the names of anyone in my family except my mom and dad. And he's dead, so he can't tell me anything."

"No one?" I asked, my gloom forgotten at this impossibility. What would it be like to know nothing about your family? Even if they were horrible, they were still family. I couldn't imagine having nobody. "Not even your grandparents?"

"If I have any," Jaslyn said with a weird kind of bravado. "I don't know if they're alive or dead, if I have cousins or anything. Mom says the past is best forgotten."

"So that's why you chose this project from Dr. Collins's list?" Incredibly, I began to understand.

"Brilliant," Jo commented. "Because it's for school, your mom will have to cooperate. That's truly brilliant, Jas."

Jas. I liked that. It was way better than Jaslyn. Suddenly, I wished I hadn't chosen a safe rellie. Both Jo and Jas's searches sounded much more interesting than mine. "Okay," I said and went over to the white board Dad had put up for the twins years ago when they kept forgetting their chores. Earlier I had written our names at the top of columns. Now I wrote WHO and then in Jo's column put "Great-grandfather" and ??? in both Jaslyn's column and mine.

"Bill," Jo said. "I'm pretty sure his name was Bill." She took the marker from me and added Bill beside "great-grandfather."

Jas was copying down my chart. "This is wonderful, Jenn. It gives us something definite to work on. Maybe we should decide to meet every Sunday, as that's the easiest. You could come here for lunch after church. Anyway, I'm going to work on Mom. Maybe by next week I'll have something to report, and all of us can fill out the first two lines on the chart. Two, at least."

Jo nodded. "I agree. It's a great chart, Jenn. Logical, and helps us see our next steps. I'll text Dad and see if he knows great-grandfather's exact name and regiment. Then I'll Google him. There has to be a lot of sites about guys who died on D-Day."

"And I'm going to ask Mom where the family records are," I said as I got to my feet. "Then I'll find out which rellie to work on and see if there's anything about her in the school library."

Proud of my plan, I went to the kitchen and found Mom and Mrs. Green making lists as well, like which plumber to use, the gardeners' phone numbers. Mom put her pen down, looked at my face, and her smile looked relieved. "Ah," she said. "Just the person I wanted to see. Mrs. Green is going to pick Mikey up on Saturday at 8:30. That should give her enough time to get him here even if the ferry's late or the bridge is jammed. His appointment is at 9:30, so they will pick you up at Leith at 9:15. That sound all right to you?"

I nodded. Mom had left lots of time. but my heart quaked at the thought of being Mikey's parent in the interviews. "You'd better pray for us," I told Mom.

She nodded. "Of course. As I do every day. Now, about the assignment. Sorted things out?"

"I never dreamed it would be so hard," I said. "My part is going to be the easiest. I'm going to study whoever was at Prim Heights during World War II. Was it GG?"

GG was what I used to call my great-grandmother. Apparently. I don't remember, because she died when I was two.

Mom took a long while before she answered. She seemed to be doing lists in her head. Then she said slowly, "I don't think anyone was in school during the war." She must have seen the look on my face because she added, "But it won't hurt to look."

Jo came into the kitchen. "Mrs. North, would you mind if I went back to school now. I've just remembered that I haven't done tomorrow's math homework. I could go now with Jas and Mrs. Green when they leave? Is that OK?"

What a whopper, I thought as I watched the three of them leave a few minutes later but I didn't mind Jo's lie about math one little bit. Mom and I would be able to say good-bye properly.

Mom and I went downstairs to the basement and as I helped her shift boxes around the box room, I saw my name on one. "Can I look at that?" I asked and, before Mom could say anything, began checking it out. All my reports cards were in it, plus the pictures I made in Grade 1—you know, the ones with the huge stick-like moms and dads and a tiny me. To my absolute surprise, my school bills from Prim Heights were also there neatly itemized. "Why are you keeping these, Mom? Do you think the school will suddenly remember you didn't pay for kindergarten?"

Mom laughed and reached for another box. Although the box itself was newish, the paper inside was yellowish and crumbling. Mom took a folder out and, to my absolute astonishment, the familiar words "Primrose Heights School for Young Ladies" were elaborately scrolled atop a piece of paper. Below was an itemized bill dated 1885 for Jennifer Anne Fraser, and I realized that I was looking at a bill from the very first term at Prim Heights. Back then tuition was $50, and my great-great-whatever grandfather paid for extras such as piano lessons ($10), equine dressage (which didn't mean dressing up horses but nevertheless cost $15), and $5 for milk and apples during break.

I felt absurdly humbled and excited. Humbled because Jennifer Anne Fraser suddenly became a little bit more real; excited by the thought of doing fancy charts, comparing the 1885 school bill to a 1940s one, and then to mine. That's my particular kind of brain-thing, one of the ways I make sense of things.

After putting the 1880s box back on the shelf, Mom pulled down another. "If we have anything, it will be in this, Jenn," she said as she blew dust off the top of the box and rummaged in it for a few moments before giving a cry of triumph. "Here we go. School bills for Jennifer Anne Lascelles." She flipped through the papers, taking so long that I wanted to reach over and grab them for myself. Finally she made a weird sound—half-satisfaction, half-disappointment. "Well," she said, handing the folder over to me. "You won't be happy. Your grandmother started at Prim Heights in September 1946. The war's over by then."

I knew Grandmother was born in 1940. "But kindergarten? Didn't she at least go to kindergarten?" I asked, grasping at straws.

"She got polio when she was three or four. It must have kept her out of school."

Grandmother's long ago polio was my last straw, and it wasn't a camel's back that broke. Instead some floodgate inside me burst, and my tears and anger exploded through it. I had tried so hard to be brave and now I couldn't. Mom quickly put the boxes back on the shelves and reached for me. She hugged me, and pulled me down to the floor where she took me into her arms as if I were two or three again. I cried and cried and, for a while, thought I'd never stop.

Finally Mom pushed me back so she could look into my eyes. "This is more than today, isn't it? The outburst, I mean. What's really bothering you, Jenn?"

I tried to burrow my way back into Mom's shoulder. "That's enough, Jenn," she said rather sternly. "Tell me what's going on. Is it just because I'm going back east tomorrow?"

I shook my head, and Mom shook me. "Then what? Jenn, you have to tell me. I can't go off and leave you like this."

Maybe there's a finite amount of tears in a person's body, or maybe Mom's shaking worked, because gradually my sobs became less ugly and quieter. As I began settling down, Mom patted my hair smooth, like she had done when I was a baby, and just like that, all my secret angst poured out. "Mom," I asked. "Why don't you want me anymore? What did I do wrong? Why are you leaving me behind?"

Mom's face showed total shock for a second, and then her eyes filled with tears. "You shouldn't be thinking like that. You've done nothing wrong, Jenn, and I'm sorry we've been careless enough to make you think that." She hugged me tight again and spoke into my shoulder. "Look, if you really want to come out east and go to school there, I'll buy the ticket when we go upstairs. But," and here she pushed me back a little again so that she could look at me, "it's ugly, Jenn. Between your dad and me, that is. About the only thing we can agree on, at the moment, is our love for you and the boys. That's something you can take to the bank."

Mom pulled me tight again and she sort of mumbled into my shoulder, "Jenn, I don't think it will work out. But, please believe me. I'm sorry, really sorry, that you thought boarding here was being abandoned. Your dad and I truly thought you'd be happier here. You have friends, teachers who know you. It wouldn't be like having to start at a new school for maybe only a few months. Do you understand?"

I scratched at a little pile of dirt on the floor while I thought. Both of us would have to change our clothes after sitting on the dusty floor, and that showed me more than Mom's words how sincere she was. I now truly believed that she and Dad thought that being a boarder would be best for me. It's hard to describe how I felt. The cliché would be that I felt like a ton of bricks had been lifted off me. Well, half a ton. In any case, I felt confident enough to ask the next question, "Mom, is there anything I can do to get Dad back? Why is he so determined to move to Toronto?"

"It's his family, Jenn. Mine has always had our girls go to Prim Heights, but I'd yank you in a moment if you weren't happy there. His is different. A North has always been the head of the firm since…" she said and stopped.

"Forever. Before God created the world," I finished.

For the first time in ages I saw Mom smile when she said, "More than like 1844. Now Uncle Gerald has cancer, Dad's mother expects Dad to drop everything and take over as managing partner. He had agreed to it before he even talked to me. It's a permanent move for him, Jenn. He won't be coming back to B.C. to live here again." Mom's lip quivered, and if she'd cried I would not have blamed her. When she went on, it was in something like a whisper, "I never dreamed I'd come second to a law firm when I married him."

"We're all coming second," I muttered, beginning to understand how Mom felt.

"Yes, you are," Mom said, as she grabbed a shelf, pulled herself to her feet and held a hand out for me. She didn't take her hand away when we walked back upstairs. In the kitchen she started making tea while I cut a tiny slice of carrot cake for each of us.

We both had sugar in our tea—something of an indulgence—but I think we needed strong tea, plus a little milk and sugar that afternoon. I had half eaten my piece of cake, when Mom became serious again. "Jenn, about your project. I know my family doesn't work, but there's always Jonathan's."

I grimaced. "Only if I had to study the American Revolution."

That was another thing about the Norths—the eastern ones, that is. They had originally come to Canada from Boston in 1784, and they prided themselves as being UELs, United Empire Loyalists. Nobody I knew in Vancouver had ever heard of the

UELs. Apparently, though, they were a big thing in Toronto.

Looking up Dad's family would be hard work, like they came from a different planet. But, surely, one of them must have fought for God, country and the UELs in World War II.

Mom interrupted my thoughts. "I've got it! she said and high-fived me. "What about the sainted Henry?"

One of the twins had christened my great-great grandfather the sainted Henry after Dad had prosed on about him once too often. In fact, if our family wasn't Anglican, I'm certain that we would have worshipped the sainted Henry instead of God.

If we lived out east, I'm sure I would have known everything about him but, as I usually zoned out when Dad started, I knew only the bare basics. He had run the family law firm until he became the most conservative politician possible. He'd been so successful at it that he'd become a cabinet minister.

Best of all he'd be in a history book somewhere. Suddenly, a little part of me became as happy as I'd been before Dad's bombshell in the summer. Tahiti wasn't a hope anymore. It was a certainty.

4

The next week was horrible. Beyond words horrible. I found a brilliant line in Romeo and Juliet: "I bite my thumb at you, sir." No one else knows it so when I can't keep the horribleness of life out of my mind, I bite my thumb at it in the way Shakespeare intended—a kind of middle finger salute.

I bit my thumb a lot this week.

It started great. My marks were in the stratosphere. Being a boarder means being bored enough to study. I could apply to Harvard right now and they'd be so impressed with my genius, they'd go down on bended knees to beg me to come. When our weekly marks were posted on Monday morning, teacher smiles were like the sun shining only on me.

I dazzled.

The weather was brilliant as well. When Jo asked

if I wanted to play tennis, it was a no-brainer. I figured we had only a couple more weeks before the real Vancouver weather of rain and more rain set in. We were in luck and got the last free court. At first we rallied back and forth. After a while I realized that while I was galloping all over the court, Jo was still in its middle as calm as water at first light. I couldn't tell if she'd even worked up a sweat or not. When she suggested a game, I thought at least I'd be able to catch my breath between serves.

How dumb could I be? It seemed like my increased classroom smarts must have made every other kind vaporize. No matter what I did, Jo just stood there sending balls wherever she wanted just by a flick of her wrist. When the tennis coach, Ms. Copeland, walked onto the court and asked if we'd play doubles, I nodded yes frantically before Jo had a chance to say anything. But when I saw the two we were to play against, I groaned.

Skirty and Flirty. They're only Grade 11s but everyone in the school knows them. Not only that but has also despised them from the time they'd transferred in. They were special and they made sure we knew it.

Prim Heights has two outstanding programs—ones parents send their female offspring right across the world for. Like, there are three girls from China, two from Korea, two from the United Arab Emirates and about ten Americans in our equestrian mini-school.

The Equestrian Centre's been around since Prim Heights started. When so many girls from up-country brought their horses with them, the school bought five hundred acres outside city limits and built a huge stable. Turned out to be one of the reasons the school became great because, when Prim Heights outgrew its original building and Vancouver real estate prices soared, they built our current school next to the old stables.

The Centre specializes in two things. A couple of our grads have won Olympic medals in show jumping and dressage. It also offers AP-like courses in animal biology. These get our girls into vet schools and are an equal attraction.

By and large, the horsey girls are fine. They're not snobs and don't look down on the rest of us like the tennis prima-donnas do.

The Tennis Academy kind of snuck into Prim Heights. It's like the Board of Governors went to sleep one day and woke up the next to find out that they'd voted it in. Of course, there's a group of people who insist the Board was drunk when the vote was made. Anyway after some 1980s parent with more money than brains said he'd fund it, that was that.

We feel kind of proud of the Equestrian Centre. It's unique and it's been around forever. But the Tennis Academy? And, if I had to pick any two players to explain why no one likes it, they'd be Skirty and Flirty.

Their names say it all.

Skirty's kilt is always a millimetre short of her crotch. We get into trouble if ours are more than twelve centimetres from our knees. She seems to skate by. Of course, the fact that she's Canadian Junior Tennis champion might blind the teachers' eyes.

I'd never actually talked to either of them, but now we had to play them. "Prepare to be humbled," I muttered to Jo.

She laughed. "I'm good with being humble."

Skirty and Flirty looked at us like we were ants that had crawled through someone's vomit. They didn't even bother warming up. Skirty strode to the net and dug a coin out of her warm-ups. "Call," she demanded.

"Tails," Jo obliged. I groaned. Didn't Jo understand that in a few short minutes we'd have our tails beaten off?

Of course we lost the toss. Everyone knows you

should call heads. Jo, however, smiled. "I always like to start on defence if I've never seen anyone play," she whispered. "I'll take the net and poach like crazy. You should be able to run everything else down."

"You think?"

Skirty made a production of taking off her warm-ups, revealing something skin-tight underneath. I kind of gaped, because I'd never seen a tennis body suit before. Next, she bounced the ball about a hundred times. She was probably trying to intimidate us, but it irritated the dickens out of me. More than that, it steeled my determination to fight when she served to me. Whatever happened, I'd get the ball back into play.

She must have irritated Jo as well, because she slammed Skirty's first serve went back faster than it had come. Skirty rolled her eyes at Ms. Copeland, as if to say beginner's luck, and that made me madder than ever. I blocked her next serve back over the net and felt that if we didn't win another point, I'd go home happy.

Jo, it turned out, had other ideas. She'd decided we wouldn't lose any points. Zero. She sent Skirty's next serve back in the same impossible-to-get place as the first. Skirty glared at Jo. She glared at me as well. I knew I was going to be the sacrificial offering. But

Jo had her thinking and she double-faulted. That was our game and it turned out, essentially our match.

Jo's serve was a blur. Nothing got by her at the net. She was incredible. Of course, she's six foot two and extremely fit, but nevertheless…

I don't follow tennis much. But I've always watched Wimbledon and the US Open finals with Mom, and it seemed to me that Jo combined the elegance of Federer with the ferocity of Rafael Nadal. Whatever she didn't knock back for a winner at the net, I dashed around putting balls I never thought I could get back into play. When we shook hands, Skirty and Flirty looked stunned. Jo and I looked at our watches, realized we'd be late for volleyball, said the obligatory "good game and thanks," and raced for the gym.

The next morning Jo was called out of class by the counsellor.

She gave me the details at lunch. "Seems there's a vacancy in the Tennis Academy," she began.

"And?"

"They offered it to me."

"Jo, the coaching fees are gazillion dollars."

"They said, seeing I'm already a Prim Heights student, there's no extra cost."

I started eating slowly. There was always a waiting

list for the Academy, and always parents willing to give their baby girl the chance to be the next tennis mega-star. Jo had to be really, really special to be offered the equivalent of a scholarship. I put my fork down and looked at her.

"And?"

Jo took her time eating the rest of her salad, munching each mouthful as though her life depended on it. She smiled, as though she knew that I was fretting, but kept eating. Finally, I couldn't stand it any longer. "And? Like in what did you say?"

"I said I'd committed to volleyball."

"That's only till November," I pointed out.

"That's what they said before they offered Skirty as a doubles partner."

I know my jaw nearly hit the floor. Jo had to be more fantastic than I'd thought for the Canadian champion to be tossed in to seal the deal. "What did Skirty say?"

Jo reached for an apple, but I pushed the bowl of fruit out of her reach. "You're not eating another mouthful until you tell me."

She shrugged and tugged the bowl towards her. "What do you think? She was all smiles while Ms. Copeland was around but, on the way back to class, she said she'd kill me first. Anyway, it didn't matter.

I'd already told Ms. Copeland that I could beat Skirty and Flirty any day with you as my partner, so why would I want to change?"

I grinned. It made my day. For a while anyway, but then I started to worry. I knew Prim Heights better than Jo, and I knew the campaign to get her to join tennis had only just began.

I hate being right. Well, I hate being right about bad things. Every day afterwards Jo was called out of class. Skirty and Flirty tried to make nice to us—a difficult task since they couldn't even spell the word. Jas asked what was going on and, after I told her, she began to worry too. If the Academy vacuum sucked Jo in, she wouldn't have time for our project. Once again, I'd be in a group with two of us doing the work of three.

The only good news that entire week was that I made the librarian happy when I asked if she could track down an old copy of the Who's Who. At first she told me to look on the internet, but when I told her that I needed an original source, she said there might be a 1930s or 1940s one in storage, If not, she promised to take me to the UBC library one day after school. Of course, during school would have been better but, with Jo either at the counsellor's office or hiding from Ms. Copeland, anything was fine.

We stayed at Leith Friday night but I made everyone miserable because I couldn't get the St. Nick's interview out of my mind. I had no idea what kinds of questions parents had to answer and no one could help me. There was only one bright light — Jo volunteered to come with me.

"We have to wear number one uniforms," I told her. Prim Heights had certain occasions, like Remembrance Day, when it was compulsory to wear blazers and a brown and blue striped tie with our kilts. The St. Nick's interview apparently counted as a number one occasion.

When Mrs. Green picked us up the next morning, I saw that Mikey was dressed up as well in his best jeans and a jacket. He grinned at me but when I introduced him to Jo he straightened his back, held his hand out and said, "Hi. I'm Mike."

So Mike it became. We arrived at St. Nick's and I led the way to the headmaster's office. Mr. Creighton came forward, hand outstretched, and after I'd introduced him to Jo and Mike, Mike was taken away for some tests and his interview. I looked at Jo and prepared for a grilling but it was easy. The secretary brought coffee and cookies in and gradually I told all that I knew about Mikey. I said that he hated the school he went to because it thought he was nothing but a dumb Indian.

"How does Mike react to that?" Mr. Creighton asked.

I thought for a while. "He's never brought school up before this year. I didn't know he was so angry about it. The thing is, sir, he's smart. Really smart. Maybe not in English, but in everything else. We always thought he might become a pro athlete because he's seems so good at everything. But since he got his money from the leasing deal all he's done is talk about coming here and learning math."

"Jenn, you know the school through your brothers. I'm sure you heard them talks about things. How do you think Mike would fit in?"

The secretary poured more coffee and Jo tried to give me a cookie but I refused. I was too nervous to eat. I decided to be honest and chose my words carefully, "I think it would depend on how much prejudice he had to face. He hides his hurt well because he didn't say anything about school until this year. I think that's because he thought there was no hope. Now he thinks he might have a good future. He doesn't have to be a fisherman like every other male in his family. I think he'll put up with a lot of name-calling because he wants this chance so badly. Besides, according to Dan and Dave, he might be the best rugby player St. Nick's has ever had."

Jo made a noise that she muffled immediately and I saw Mr. Creighton's lips twitch. I knew I was being shameless but I loved Mikey so why not hit St. Nick's where it counted — its rugby team.

"Thank you for being so honest, Jenn. Is there anything else you'd like to add?"

I thought hard. Education was a tough sell for many First Nations kids on the island. The benefits seemed so far away. I really believed Mikey deserved this chance but I'd said just about everything. "Sir," I said eventually. "Please. If there's any chance for him, let him know so that he'll go back to his regular school and work hard for next year. Give him hope."

Mr. Creighton stood and I knew the interview was over. I had no idea if I'd hurt or helped Mikey but I'd given it my best shot. Mr. Creighton's secretary escorted us out and then asked Jo if she'd like to see over the school while Mikey had his interview. I said I knew the school pretty well so if she was busy I could take Jo on the tour. We skipped the classrooms but Jo marvelled at the Olympic-sized swimming pool and the number of rugby fields. Our tennis courts were better, naturally, but everything else seemed pretty much a toss-up.

When we headed back to Mr. Creighton's office, Mike greeted us with a wide smile. He had enjoyed himself. The tests had been okay but the math one had been harder than he expected. Mr. Creighton put his hand on Mike's shoulder, "I enjoyed meeting you, Mike. You will hear from us, one way or another, within a week. You have my word on that."

We all said our good-byes but Mike's smile didn't change. Mrs. Green picked us up and we gave Mike a quick tour of Prim Heights and then they waited outside Leith while Jo and I changed clothes and picked up our tennis racquets. I felt like I'd escaped something when we all sat down for lunch at my house. When Mrs. Green left to drive Mike back to the ferry terminal, Jo suggested tennis on the courts in the park. I jumped at the chance to pound my anger out on yellow tennis balls and we turned to Jas but she said she always had dance class on Saturday afternoons. We said we'd drop by and maybe go onto a movie or something.

Dance at Prim Heights is still evolving from the cotillion stage so I didn't know what to expect when we entered the dance studio. One thing I saw straightaway was that Jas was terrific. Confident. Sexy. I didn't know what to call her style of dance but Jo said it was contemporary. Anyway, Jas was so different from the Jaslyn Green I knew from school or Youth Group that I wondered how she managed to wash that confidence off in the showers.

Over supper that night we tried to make Mrs. Green understand about Ms. Copeland pressurizing Jo.

"Since when is tennis so important in Canada?" she asked.

"Never," I answered with assurance. Emilie Bouchard, but other than her, I couldn't remember any great female player.

"It's the Australian thing," Jo said, and her voice sounded angry. "They dug up my records from there and found out I was a national age class champion. What's worse, they're using all the arguments my old school made. I had to play tennis there because I was too young to say no. Here I can, and I've said it till I'm sick of my own voice. I don't want to be a tennis pro. I don't want to specialize. I want to try a bunch of new things. That's why I'm in Comp Sports in the first place."

Mrs. Green still looked bewildered. "What does your father say?"

Jo's look changed to frustration. "I want him to back me up and tell Ms. Copeland where to go, but he says it's a fantastic opportunity and I should think about it."

Jas intervened. "Come on. Let's get the dishes done and find something on Netflix."

After we'd finished, supper I let Jas and Jo canter downstairs to the family room before I went to Mrs. Green's sitting room. I mean, my mom's old sitting room. After I knocked, Mrs. Green looked surprised. "You should know you don't have to knock in your own house, Jenn. Does it feel so weird?"

I felt tears coming into my eyes as I nodded. "It will take time," she told me.

I nodded again. "Mrs. Green," I began hesitantly. "About Mom. With all the tennis stuff, I didn't realise that I haven't heard from her. Not really, that is. I've had a couple of texts and tweets, but they don't say anything. Has she phoned or emailed you?"

"Just once to tell me about Thanksgiving. Don't worry, Jenn. She said she'd call this weekend."

I tried phoning Mom before I went to bed and finally got through the next morning. After the usual pleasantries, I told her about Jo's tennis and its problems.

"She should decide for herself," Mom said, but her voice sounded tight, like she was talking with an uncooperative lady on one of her committees.

"How's Toronto?" I asked. "Are you settling in?"

There was an ominous silence before Mom told me that TO was fine. Sure, I said to myself, and I can beat Jo at tennis. Any time Mom used TO for Toronto that meant trouble. To change to a happier topic, I asked Mom if she knew when she and Dad would arrive back for Thanksgiving.

The silence stretched longer this time, and when Mom spoke, her voice had a brittle tone that I had never heard before. "Ah," she finally said. "Dad and I have decided that it would be easier for everyone if you came here. That way you can see Dan and Dave."

Easier for Dad, I translated. I listened to Mom tell me that Mrs. Green would get me to the airport, but all the time my stomach roiled. I knew that Mom had just told me that Dad wouldn't ever come here, to our house again. Ever.

I didn't know what that meant. Would I have to go to the school with the weird collars after all? Were Mom and Dad really getting a divorce? Would Mom live here or there? Would I always be a boarder and have to fly across the country just to see my parents?

We all shuffled off to church Sunday morning and after lunch we went downstairs to our "war room." Jo reported first. Somehow, when she wasn't hiding from Coach Copeland, she'd managed to build up a dossier on her great-grandfather Bill. She showed us photos of his grave in Normandy, France and his page in Canada's Roll of Honour. She'd also emailed someone at the National Archives in Ottawa to see if she could get the record of what he did in the war.

I had nothing as magnificent as that to offer. I told them about my epiphany with the librarian, but Jas interrupted.

"Why do you have to go to UBC? What's wrong with Wikipedia?"

"Wikipedia's sometimes has mistakes and it's not a primary source. *Who's Who* is, and that means extra marks, remember? I'll be able to tell you much more next week."

"Scout's honour?" Jo asked, and I held up two fingers.

We laughed, and then it was Jas's turn. She slumped in her chair and looked defeated. The difference between yesterday's dancer and right now was mind-blowing.

"Mom says I should get another project," she said eventually.

"Why?" Jo asked.

"She says there's nothing but heartbreak if I keep doing this."

"Does she explain why?" Jo asked in a much gentler voice.

"She said they wouldn't speak to Dad after he married her, so why would they speak to me now?"

I don't think either Jo or I knew exactly what to say, but I had one question. "Who *are* they?"

Jas looked around the room as though she was trying to find a way out. "Relatives? I don't know. Mom just gave me an address in Toronto. That's when she said there'd be nothing but heartache."

"Whereabouts in Toronto?"

"Some place called Rosedale."

I got excited. "But that's where Mom and Dad are. I don't know how big it is. Maybe they've met."

Jas shrugged, Jo went upstairs to the kitchen to get some snacks, and I poured fresh tea into our cups. When Jo came back down, she looked at me, and I could see that she'd had much the same idea as I'd had.

"I've just found out that I have to go east for Thanksgiving," I began.

"It doesn't seem right to have Thanksgiving in October," Jo interrupted. "It should be near Christmas."

"And just when did you have it in Australia?" Jas asked, turning on Jo like she was an enemy.

"Children," I said in the patronizing kind of voice

Mom used with her committees. "Let's not get side-tracked. I've been thinking. Jo, if your dad and my mom spring us out of jail a day or so early, I could go to Ottawa and help you research. Then, maybe, you and your dad might like to have Thanksgiving dinner in Toronto with my family. That way we travel across the country together. We can tell our parents it's safer that way."

I caught Jas's envious look. "You're welcome too, Jas, but I'm sure your mom wants you here."

She nodded gloomily and didn't notice the looks Jo and I exchanged. If things worked out, I'd have Jo alongside me when I went to that address in Toronto. Together we might find out something about Jas's father. The way I looked at it, even if we failed, we couldn't make matters any worse for the Green family.

5

As soon as we got back to Leith House, Mrs. Sinclair handed Jo an envelope. "I was asked to give you this asap," she explained.

To my surprise, Jo didn't open it immediately. Instead she tossed it on her bed and proceeded to get kilted and shirted for chapel. Once suitably attired, she picked it up again and tossed it over to me. "What do you think? Methinks I smell a very persistent rat."

The envelope was the size that birthday cards came in but of much better quality, and Jo's name was beautifully inscribed in italic lettering. I, too, smelled a rat and wondered what Ms. Copeland was up to. "Come on, open it," I told her as I buttoned up my shirt. "Let's get the news now. If it's bad, we can pray about it in chapel."

The news wasn't bad. I gasped when I saw an invitation that a lot of girls lusted after—not just in Prim Heights but girls in every other Vancouver school.

The St. Nick's tennis team hosted a dinner dance every year as a fundraiser. It was strictly adults only—except for the tennis players and their dates. There were twelve guys on the team, so twelve possible dates. Twelve dates and thousands and thousands of girls.

I'd never seen an invitation before and, truth to tell, had never wanted one. I'd met a couple of the tennis guys when Dave and Dan were at St. Nick's and thought they were snobs.

I tried to tell Jo some of this after she'd tossed the invite into the bin. "You could sell it, you know. Celeste Pepin would probably give you a thousand bucks for it."

Jo retrieved it immediately. "Do you want it?"

I tossed it back into the bin. "What do you think? But I can tell you one thing. If Ms. Copeland goes on like this, I'm going to enjoy the next couple of weeks."

Actually, the only thing that made the next couple of weeks endurable was that Mom got in touch with Jo's dad and made fantastic plans. They were pulling us out of school for an entire week. Mom would go with us to Archives Canada to make sure we got what we needed and she was even working on getting access to the actual office great-great grandfather Henry worked in when he was a cabinet minister.

On Thanksgiving Saturday all of us would make the short flight from Ottawa to Toronto. While Jo and her dad stayed in a hotel, Mom and I would go to Dad's new house just down the street from the North family mansion. I was semi-delighted about that. On one hand I wouldn't be staying with Attila, the Huness. On the other hand, a house down the street from my grandmother sounded awfully permanent.

The best news of all was that we'd arrive back in Vancouver the day before the dinner dance. "There's your excuse," I told Jo. "Just tell Coach that. She'll understand jet-lagged."

Understand was a word Ms. Copeland had failed to learn. "She says she'll pick me up at the airport," Jo reported back.

The only other blind determination I'd ever seen before was Dad's devotion to his side of the family. I felt the familiar bitter taste of defeat come into my mouth as I made the comparison. "What on earth did you say to that?"

Jo smiled. "I said I'd only go if you got an invitation too."

Like I said, invitations to the thing were like hen's teeth. Scarce. I had no idea how Ms. Copeland had wrangled Jo's, but I knew there was no chance she could rustle up another one for me. Parents and their friends paid at least $1000 for just one ticket. I knew I wasn't worth that. At least, not to Ms. Copeland.

The following day Coach Copeland taught me the folly of underestimating her, and I figured out just why her programme was so successful. She was relentless. Just before the final bell, both Jo and I were called out of class to meet two of the cutest guys imaginable. They smiled as they handed me an identical envelope to Jo's and then asked permission to pick us up in a limo for the dance.

Jo and I looked at each other. I couldn't look at them because they'd see the drool on my face. But I was angry for Jo. She was being harassed and hounded into doing something she didn't want to do.

"I don't know what to say," I eventually stammered. "I'll have to ask my father and I won't see him until Thanksgiving."

One of the boys whipped out his cell. "Phone him now."

My eyes bulged. "And interrupt his dinner? That's a surefire no," I blurted out and then kicked myself. I'd just passed up a perfect opportunity to refuse the invitation. Still, it wouldn't hurt to put Dad in touch with Ms. Copeland. I couldn't imagine a more perfect pair.

Jo and I talked about it as we walked home to Leith House after volleyball. "What are we going to do?"

"Look for dresses in Toronto," she answered. "What a perfect excuse to get Dad's credit card into a shop."

"And then?"

"And then I'm going to milk this thing as long as I can. I've told Ms. Copeland that I'm not interested. I've said I don't want to be hounded, that I won't play tennis this year, but if she keeps giving me bribes like this, I'll keep taking the bribes. Eventually, of course, Dad will have to put his foot down and make up some excuse, like it's distracting me from settling into my new school. Whatever. The more she goes on and on about this, the more I don't want to play."

But when Jas saw the tickets, she couldn't keep the longing out of her eyes, and I remembered the Jas from her dance studio. Jo didn't say anything but next day, after lunch, she gruffly handed yet another ticket to Jas. "Don't lose it," she said. "You know how precious they are."

As we walked home, I couldn't help asking, "How precious was that ticket exactly?"

Jo blushed. "I compromised. A bit. I told Coach, I'd really think about it if she backed off and got Jas a ticket." Jo swallowed a bit, and her voice was soft but rough when she continued, "You and I have it good, Jenn. I know things are dirt between your Mom and Dad but other than that, you have it made. Me too."

Sometimes when I thought about Jas and Mrs. Green I felt guilty. Most of the time I took my life for granted. Prim Heights had far richer families than mine. But I was now in Grade 9 and starting to think and change my mind about things. I'd sneered at Jas going to Disney World. Now I wondered about asking if she wanted to come to QBeach for a couple of weeks next summer.

Jo was obviously thinking along the same lines because her voice sounded angry when she went on. "As I said, you and I have it easy. But Jas? There's some huge problem with her family. She doesn't know anything about her father and her mom works so hard to give her anything. We're going to buy the prettiest dresses Toronto has to offer. Mrs. Green will probably stay up all hours to make sure Jas looks stunning. When you think about it, the ticket was easy. Worst case scenario? You and I have to play a few doubles games with each other."

If I were a guy, I think I would have fallen irretrievably in love with Jo at that point.

After most of the class left on Wednesday, Kimberley, don't-call-me Kim, Leung and her friends cornered me. You've heard of Asian mothers? Well, Mrs. Leung is their queen. If anyone hated the loss of Mrs. Robinson more than me, it was Kimberley. She had worked just as hard as I had during the summer if not harder. I would have felt sorry for her, if she hadn't been the school's biggest whiner.

Until the Zhous moved to New York, my best friends had been Asian so I knew something about Kimberley and her group. Forget getting into Stanford, Pomona, or Duke. Mrs. Leung had decided that her daughter would go to either Cambridge, UK or Cambridge, USA., as in Harvard. Oxford and Yale were unacceptable. Part of the Cambridge thing was that nobody from Prim Heights had been accepted there for about a decade. And Harvard? No need to explain that.

Therefore, getting the top mark in every class was more important to Kimberley than breathing and, as I said, she was the school's top whiner. Every sentence seemed to begin with "It's not fair," and this afternoon was no exception. "It's not fair," she began, as one of her underlings pinched my arm. "You shouldn't be allowed to go to the Archives in Ottawa. You're only doing it so show everyone how great you are." Pinch, pinch and yet another on my other arm for good measure. "Just because you're Jennifer Anne, descended from the original Jennifer Anne, you get away with everything."

"So not fair," Myra Wang added.

"Plus, her Mom's on the Board of Governors," Patti Cheng said, putting in her two bits worth.

"You think the world revolves around you," Kimberley declared, returning to the attack. "My mother's getting up a petition demanding that you can't use anything you found at the Archives. Nobody else can go there so you'll have an unfair advantage."

"Like Dr. Collins will be impressed with that? I don't think so, Kim," I said as I twisted myself away from the pack. "Go and play mall shopping," I told them, making a shooing motion. "And, Kimberley? Tell your mother to stop dreaming about Cambridge, Massachusetts or Cambridge, England. You're going local. Nobody else will have you."

I let that sink in for a moment and then poked her chest with my finger to pound the point home as I said, "Jaslyn Green, Jo Carruthers and I are getting the top Humanities mark. And when we've done that, we'll just work a tiny bit harder and come top in everything else. Your mother won't be able to stop us."

I walked out of the classroom, and a couple of other girls ran after me. "Oh my goodness. You told her. That's exactly what she needs to hear," one said.

"I am so sick of Mrs. Leung complaining about everything," another said and tried to high-five me.

I looked at them. Where had they been when my arms were getting pinched and twisted? I knew that Jo would have taken Kimberley on in a heartbeat, and I was beginning to believe that Jas would have been there too, in her own fierce way. I was so glad they were in my group.

I was even more ecstatic that I wouldn't have to go back to school for an entire week, but that didn't stop me from deleting my attackers from all my social media sites as soon as I got back to Leith. Then we met Mrs. Green and left to catch our plane.

I don't know which of us screamed the loudest, Jo or me, when we saw our parents waiting for us at the Ottawa airport. I do know that I hugged Mom like there was no tomorrow and she only pulled away when the baggage carousel started. Mr. Carruthers was just like Jo, friendly, charming, and quietly knowledgeable. He and Mom must have made some serious phone calls, because they'd mapped our entire Ottawa schedule out for us.

He took us out for dinner. I felt vaguely disappointed with my prawn linguini. I could have had it in Vancouver, it was so generic. I wondered what a genuine Ottawa meal would be. When Mom saw me grin at some of the meals I was conjuring up—like crow with blackberry sauce—she made me tell everyone what I'd been thinking.

They laughed.

"Politicians should eat crow all the time," Mr. Carruthers told me.

"With no seasonings or sauces," Jo added.

"But what about regular people? It's so cold here in the winter. Maybe there should be a special redhot Ottawa chili," Mom argued. "But before I forget. I've got news. There's a huge surprise waiting for you back in Vancouver. St. Nick's accepted Mike."

Jo smiled and I pumped my fist and said, "I hoped so hard but I didn't really think he had a chance."

Mom beamed at me. "Mr. Creighton told me Mike has a lot to thank you for. You did an excellent job, Jenn. But Mike did as well. The most extraordinary part though is that he's entering Grade 7 this year. He'll have to work really hard of course but he knows that."

"They must think he's going to be a great rugby player," Jo said.

Mom frowned and shook her head. "That's what I would have thought too but it's not that. It's his math. They gave him a multi-grade test and he only had trouble with some of the senior AP level stuff. They think he's some kind of prodigy."

"I told Mr. Creighton he was smart but I didn't think he was that smart."

It felt so strange to be in the middle of uncomplicated, family-type conversation and I couldn't wait to see Dad on Sunday. Would he be my same dad? I hoped not. I desperately wanted him to have missed us, our family, and our house in Vancouver. I hoped he'd learned to put us ahead of his work but I'd take the old "I'm too busy to have time for you" dad if I had to.

I definitely did NOT want a Toronto dad.

Although I'd fallen asleep on Ottawa time, Mom had trouble getting me up and I was grumpy at breakfast. Suddenly, the archives became a fear-object. Why should I, a ninth grader, think I'd be welcome there? Was I as arrogant as Kimberley said and was using the archives instead of Google to prove my importance? I think that if Jo's great-grandfather's records were anywhere else, I would have asked Mom to take me to Toronto right then and there.

I felt even more apprehensive as Mr. Carruthers drove past the Parliament Buildings and then the Supreme Court of Canada. This was really high nose country but I felt better when he pulled up in front of the Archives Canada building. It was squat, sort of ugly, and somehow far more approachable.

That was my first surprise of the day.

I'd thought the archives would be like a library. Like, after you'd found what you wanted in the catalog, you could walk to the right shelf and find it. Wrong, wrong, wrong. First, we had to register and get security-tagged. Next I found out that while the archives building was in Ontario, the actual stuff was stored in Quebec. So the process went like this. You wrote what you wanted on a form, took it to an archivist who checked that your numbers were right and then she put it into a computer. After that you waited for it to be trucked across the Ottawa River. Usually, the wait was twenty-four hours, sometimes, forty-eight until, finally, you got to look at what you'd ordered.

Go figure. The building in one province; the precious papers in another.

But my brilliant Mom had figured this out and preordered Jo's great-grandfather's military records and the North Family Papers for me. An archivist, Ms. Kennedy, was more than willing to explain everything.

She handed Jo a dusty box, about fifteen inches wide and a foot high. "Here you go," she said. "The records of William Carstarphen Stewart." Jo looked weird. I don't think she'd ever heard her great-grandfather's middle name before. She took the box, walked over to a desk near the windows, opened her computer and got herself set up.

Then Ms. Kennedy turned to me. "I'm sorry, Jenn, but Henry North's government records and correspondence are out being digitalized. The good news is that they'll be on the web this time next year."

I frowned. Had I come here to waste time and go home without knowing anything more about the sainted Henry than I could find on my computer? How Kimberley Leung would love that!

Ms. Kennedy must have worked out what I was thinking. "Don't worry. There's still more material than you'll know what to do with. I've had his personal records brought over. There's a set of diaries in them. Now, these boxes," she said, pointing to four fat boxes on the trolley's top shelf, "are the earliest North records we have. One goes back to the 1760s."

Jo had walked away with just one box. I was now the possessor of a trolley full of them. Mom laughed at my face. "You don't know it but you got off lucky, Jenn. Ms. Kennedy said she'd need at least fifteen trolleys if everything was available." She helped me wheel the large cart to a table near Jo. "Now, where do you want to start?"

I didn't know. It felt overwhelming. Jo had already begun reading a sheet of paper. As I watched, she frowned and beckoned to Mom. "I don't understand anything. Can you help me? Everything's abbreviated. Like, SOS, TOS, VAC and L.O."

Mom laughed. "Jo, I don't even understand some of your tweets. But, I'll try. SOS means help me – literally, save our souls. That's a start."

Jo frowned again. "I don't think that's what it means here, Mrs. North," she said. "Look."

Mom studied the sheet of paper for a while. "You're right, and that means I can't help you. You'd better ask Ms. Kennedy."

While Mom looked at William Carstarphen Stewart's file, I chose the North box with the earliest date. It was much thicker than Jo's, and impossibly dirty which seemed weird because I had to wear white gloves. Inside it were bundles of paper, most tied with thin, faded bits of red tape. I untied one and unfolded a huge sheet of parchment with globs of red sealing wax all over it.

"Mom, Mom," I whispered and beckoned her over.

She looked at the sheet for some seconds and then said. "Unbelievable. This is the deed to the land Jonathan North got when he came up from Boston."

Sure enough. The words "Jonathan North" were in huge capital letters. Mom continued to puzzle over the deed. "Good grief," she said eventually, "no wonder the family's so rich. They got about half of Toronto."

They did? "Why?"

"Because they fought for King George III and not George Washington I," she answered somewhat sarcastically. "Jonathan was a colonel in the Boston militia and postmaster general there. Something like that. The land's his reward for giving that up and moving to Canada."

While Mom continued to puzzle over the deed, I looked at other things in the box. There were a lot of paper folders. In one, I found a lottery ticket. I couldn't believe my eyes. I wasn't allowed to buy lotto tickets but, Jonathan, the great ancestor, had paid five silver shillings for the small rectangular piece of paper in front of me. He might even have won but he'd been tarred and feathered and run out of town before he could claim any prize.

I wondered if it was still valid. With interest and everything, the ten Pound payout would be a considerable amount of dollars. "Mom," I said, semi-seriously, "can I go to Boston and see if it's worth anything."

"In your dreams, Jenn. In any case, the ticket belongs to the archives."

I lost interest after that. I rummaged around again and found an old silk bag. It might have been blue originally but it had faded to a dull bluish grey. I carefully opened it and stared at an old book.

It was small. Really small, like about four inches by three, and thick as well. The only other book I'd seen like that was an old Bible. But what was brilliant about this book was the bloodstained broken arrow that went halfway through it.

I beckoned Jo over. "Look at this!"

Mom put the white gloves on again and carefully picked the book up. "It's a complete Shakespeare."

"Cool," Jo said in a hushed, reverential-like voice. "Very cool."

I peeked into it. "Listen to this," I said. "James Northe, Mom. North with an e North, Boston, 1761."

I'd never heard of a James North, with or without an e. For the first time, I felt a twinge of pride in my North ancestry. More than two hundred and fifty years ago, James Northe of Boston must have had an encounter somewhere with a warlike aboriginal. Maybe a Mohawk or a Mohican.

Mom pulled another folder from the box. "There's a letter James wrote to his wife Eliza in May 1761. I wonder if it was written before or after the arrow."

We looked, but couldn't read it. Both its English and writing were incomprehensible.

"There's Ms. Kennedy," Jo told us. "I bet she can understand it."

We took it over to the archivist. She smiled and remarked, "You're just in time. I was about to go back to my Quebec office."

When she saw the letter, she gave it the kind of look teenage fans give their idols. "Wonderful," she said eventually.

"What does it say?" I asked. "We couldn't read it."

"That's partly because esses sometimes look like effs," she said. "But it is truly amazing. I'd forgotten we had this. I've been racking my brains, looking for a project for my intern, and this was here all the time. I'll tell him to make it a website feature."

By this time, she had taken us back into an office

where we could talk normally, not in the hushed voices we had to use in the Reading Room. Everywhere I looked there were boxes, and I couldn't help wondering what other treasures might be in them.

"But, Ms. Kennedy, can't you just give us some idea of what he wrote?" I pleaded.

She looked more carefully at the letter. "It's sent to his wife. He says he loves her. She'd given him the book as a birthday present. He tells her the arrow stopped exactly where Osric says to Hamlet, 'A hit, a very palpable hit,' and how blessed he felt that someone wasn't telling her that it had been a deadly hit. He'd been surveying French outposts and, oh...," she stopped to catch breath, and her face was lit by excitement. "This is so amazing. He'd escaped the French somewhere in the Vermont mountains and thought he was safe. That's when he was ambushed."

I remembered something from Dr. Collins's history lessons. "The French and Indian War? He was in that?" Suddenly history came alive, and the French and Indian War wasn't just an old fact any more.

Mom looked at me and I think my face must have been lit with the same excitement as Ms. Kennedy's, because Mom smiled as she said to her, "Maybe your intern could send us a copy when he's finished working on it."

"I'll make sure he does," Ms. Kennedy said. "But Mrs. North, you'll have to pay for it. You know how the government's pinching each penny nowadays."

As Mom settled things with Ms. Kennedy, I looked at her and got another shock. Not as big as the one I'd had with James North, nor as welcome, but a shock nonetheless.

6

Mom had changed. They'd Toronto-ized her. I'd been too excited last night and too grumpy this morning to see it. After Ms. Kennedy said that it might take six months to get the letter deciphered, Mom became icy. "It's for a term paper, Ms. Kennedy. We need it in six weeks. For Christmas, not Easter," she said, in a way that made everyone know she had money and power. I'd seen other girls' mothers act that way, but never thought Mom would.

I nearly cried. *Oh, Mom*, I thought, *what's happened?*

For the first time I wondered if a divorce might be the only thing. Obviously, Mom was getting eaten up by the current situation and I could now understand that Mom and Dad had truly protected me by making me board at Prim Heights. I hadn't believed them in the summer because I was too busy thinking

I was being punished for causing their break-up. Now that I'd got into boarding, I have to admit I really enjoyed it. I had fun and Jo was the friend I'd wanted all my life.

When I turned my attention back to Mom and Ms. Kennedy, the archivist had apparently agreed to a four week deadline, but I'm sure it was at an exorbitant cost. She'd obviously seen my "new" Mom before in other people, because she smirked when she said, "Now, about photocopying. If Jenn needs anything done to take home with her, she should have it marked and on the desk by three o'clock."

I was glad that the smirk didn't extend to me. Ms. Kennedy was patience itself as she explained how to put markers in the folders to show what I needed. Some, I was relieved to find out, I could copy the old-fashioned way by putting coins into a machine.

Reluctantly I put the boxes of early treasures to one side. Ms. Kennedy had mentioned great-great grandfather's diaries and I began searching for them. Of course, I didn't look for the right thing. I sort of expected something like a leather book with a lock on it like I'd seen at school. When I couldn't find that, I looked for anything with a leather cover. Finally I found a collection of old exercise books.

I leafed through them wondering where to start.

The good news was that I could read the writing all right. The bad? I needed to know everything about the sainted Henry's life for them to make sense. They had cryptic abbreviations everywhere. Seems every generation abbreviates. I could well imagine someone, a hundred years from now, trolling through tweets that had magically survived and trying to work lol and btw out.

I found the book for 1944 and opened it, hoping to find Henry's comments on D-Day. Maybe there would be something miraculous — like a mention of Jo's great-granddad.

Instead, something torn from a newspaper fell out—a cartoon. It must have been funny in the day, but it made no sense now. It showed a man in a suit, obviously the sainted Henry, running around in a room full of nuns. The caption read, "How many is too many, Henry?"

I stared at it for a long time. I had no idea what it meant.

I must have looked stupid because Jo came over and plopped herself beside me. "What's got you looking so puzzled?"

"This." I handed the cartoon over. "What do you think it means?"

She looked at it and grinned, "The sainted Henry got caught having sex with nuns? Who knew?"

It wasn't about sex. That I knew. It was religion. From everything I'd been taught by Dad, the sainted Henry would never be caught dead in the same room as a nun. He was Anglican; they were Catholic. In his mind, it was as simple as east and west. Oil and water. You get the point.

Jo, though, was happy. In the few short hours I'd spent with the North boxes, she'd found everything she needed from William C. Stewart's military record. A genealogical archivist had explained what the initials meant, and Jo had decoded everything from the time he walked into recruiting office till the day he died.

"There's a huge library downstairs. It's like Canada's Library of Congress. If you're not finished, I can go down there and read up on D-Day so that I understand it."

She was going to do background reading, and I'd barely started?

The problem with the sainted Henry was that his life couldn't be as easily worked out as William Carstarphen Stewart's had been. From what I gathered, Henry North spent most of his time in parliament or committees. To add even less to the mystery of the man, I understood most of the abbreviations in his diary. Like mtg, for example.

I put the diary down. It was more a planner than a cache of his thoughts on anything.

I started to hate my term project. What would I say? "During World War II, my great-great grandfather was Minister of Immigration and he went to meetings and sat in parliament."

Jo's great-grandfather had served king and country. The sainted Henry had only served the interests of those people who had voted for him.

That was one thing the diary revealed. He always had time to show people around the Parliament Buildings or have breakfast with them. But he was my relative, and I was stuck with him. At the very least I could say that he voted to support the troops and wrote letters of sympathy to widows when their husbands were KIA—killed in action.

After some time, I discovered something else. He was also Minister of Mining. That meant he travelled around the country a lot, making sure quotas were met, so that weapons could be made to help us win the war. Well, I thought, that was positive. I could say something like, "Well, my great-great grandfather didn't do anything dramatic or heroic. He worked behind the scenes, making sure that iron ore and coal were mined, so that the soldiers had weapons to fight with." That sounded much, much better than just sitting in parliament or on committees.

I flicked through the rest of 1944, then 1943, but didn't see anything. But, who knew? 1942 might be different.

As they said in the day, it sure was.

For the first time, Great-great grandfather used his 1942 diary to vent.

He'd had breakfast with a couple of men from the Canadian Jewish Congress who had urged him to admit more Jewish refugees into the country. "They don't understand," he'd fumed in the diary. "How many more times do I have to tell them? Canada doesn't need more Jews. We need farmers, miners, and loggers. Jews only settle in the big cities, set up shops and drive the other shopkeepers out of business. We've got more than enough Jew shopkeepers, as it is."

A couple of days later he ranted again. A reporter found out about the breakfast with the Jewish Congress and had caught Henry off guard. Great-great grandfather's pen spluttered blots of ink when he wrote: "The idiot had the temerity to ask exactly how many Jewish refugees I was prepared to let into Canada. I told him not too many. He asked, 'How many is too many?' and I told him in no uncertain terms that none is too many."

None is too many? The sainted Henry, whose family revered his memory, wouldn't let Jewish refugees into Canada during the time of the holocaust?

I couldn't believe it so I read on. For a couple of weeks, it was just bland, ordinary stuff like the other diaries had been. Then I saw another inkblot and, sure enough, he'd returned to the Jewish refugee thing again.

This time he vented because a Toronto newspaper had published a cartoon showing him capering, his word, not mine, around a room full of nuns. "Damnably outrageous," he'd written and underlined it three times.

A couple of days later, he was venting again. He'd gone to his lawyer's to see if he could sue the cartoonist but been told it was "fair comment." That really set him off. "How can it be fair?" he stormed. "Doesn't anyone realize that I have the welfare of an entire country at heart. I cannot afford to be swayed by stories about a few pitiful Jews and their situation."

There it was. In his own handwriting. The great and much decorated Henry North, M.P., was a bigot and a racist.

I was glad Mom and Jo were downstairs in the

library. I felt like I'd turned to stone. At a time when millions of Jews were being gassed in prison camps, my great-great grandfather wouldn't let any who'd managed to escape come to Canada.

What was he thinking? Being in cabinet, he would have had access to the latest intelligence from Europe. Surely, by 1943, word would have trickled out about Auschwitz and its counterparts. How could he have gone to church each Sunday and listened to sermons about the love of God when he didn't have any for his fellow man?

I really hadn't known much about the Norths, except for family propaganda, before now. I knew about Jonathan, but not James. Jonathan, the family's founding father in Canada, was mentioned in history books. Henry, though, was monstrously important in comparison. His bio was pages and pages long.

When it all came down to it, I didn't think I'd like either of them.

I often thought I'd like to meet all the Jennifer Annes who went to Prim Heights. We'd have school in common, for one thing. We could talk about uniforms and silly school rules. My female ancestors seemed human. Jonathan and Henry North were important men in history. Somewhat like Henry VIII.

I certainly didn't want to meet him, and now I didn't want to meet any North ancestors.

Except James. He'd loved Eliza. Did Dad love Mom?

I looked at the clock, stirred my bones, and went to the archives office. Good news. I was allowed to photocopy up to fifty pages from the 1942 diary. I got $10 worth of quarters and hit the machines.

Everyone was in a great mood that night at supper, and no one noticed that I wasn't saying anything. Truth to tell, the inattention was mutual. When Mom told me to be dressed and ready for breakfast at seven-thirty, I looked at her and said, "Seven thirty? I don't need to get up that early."

"You haven't been listening, have you?" Mom responded. "By the time we get to Montreal…"

"Montreal?"

Mr. Carruthers shook his head. "You really haven't been listening. Jenn, Montreal's a couple of hours away. I thought we could drive and then I'd either show you around or you could hunt for dresses to wear at that fancy dance."

"We'd be away all day," I said, trying to keep hysteria out of my voice. I thought frantically and turned to Mom, "If I were super-careful, could I stay here and go to the archives? I need a couple more hours to finish up."

Mom frowned. "I thought you had finished." She shook her head. "This isn't like you, Jenn. In any case, they're closed on Saturdays."

"Only the offices," I corrected. "The building's open all day. If you have stuff in the lockers, you can go in and work on it."

"And I bet you have stuff in lockers," Jo contributed, looking left out.

I realized then that I'd put everything away when she and Mom were downstairs. Somehow I'd assumed we'd be coming back.

Mom got up from the table with a sigh. She kissed Jo and smiled at Mr. Carruthers. "You'll excuse us, I hope. Jenn and I are on different wavelengths right now. I'll call you later."

Neither of us talked until we got back into our hotel room. Then Mom looked at me. "So what's so all-important about going back to the archives tomorrow? Judging from the mound of Xerox, I thought you'd have everything you need. Think about shopping in Montreal, Jenn. Why on earth would you want to do miss that?"

I couldn't explain my need to understand Henry. I didn't really understand it myself. I had four more diaries to look through, and I'd kept back two of the very early North Family boxes. I used them as an excuse. "Mom, I've got a chance to know everything about the Norths before I see Attila-ess on Sunday. For once in my life, I might know something about the family that she doesn't. She might stop seeing me as a piece of slime crawling out of a bog and we might actually talk. It's my one chance to impress her. Please?"

Mom sighed and I realized only then that she really wanted to go shopping in Montreal. Not for me. For herself. I knew I shouldn't hold her back. "Mom," I said, "you can drop me off before you leave and ask the commissioners to arrange for a taxi back here when I'm done. They're ex-cops and army officers. They won't let anything happen."

Mom sighed again. Clearly, I'd tempted her. I wanted her to be happy, especially after her non-Mom behaviour to Ms. Kennedy. I felt like I was on a teeter-totter. Against Mom's shopping, there was my need to find out if the not-so-sainted Henry had second thoughts once everyone found out about the fate of the Jews and other "undesirables" in the holocaust.

Neither of us was acting normally. Mom usually didn't have a manic need to shop. I was the shopaholic in the family. When I thought about it, I had enough material for my report. It was only my intense need to know if Henry repented and deserved Dad's adulation that drove me. I opened my mouth to tell Mom I'd happily go to Montreal when the phone rang.

Mr. Carruthers had a solution. A friend worked on his genealogical tree in the archives every Saturday. He'd be willing to "babysit" and bring me back to the hotel.

Mom's wide smile made me swallow any faint resentment about being babysat. I watched her as she phoned room service and asked them to prepare a box lunch for me and couldn't help wondering what Mr. Carruthers had that Dad didn't.

Dad's determination to put his job first seemed like the finger that flicked the first domino over. After he'd quit on Tahiti so many things changed — just like a row of dominos did once the first one fell.

Like Mom. What would have happened if Dad had said something like, "I can't give you the three weeks in Tahiti, but how about three long weekends in Paris?" Or New York? Even Montreal? Would that kind of willingness to give a little have saved my family?

I didn't know. I also didn't know the emotions I went to bed with. My illustrious ancestor somehow made me feel guilty and deeply ashamed of him. Had he changed his mind once all the Nazi secrets came out? He could have saved people. Didn't he care? It took a long time to get to sleep. I felt guilty even if Henry hadn't and that guilt made my stomach churn like it was making bitter Nazi ice cream.

The next day's reading didn't make me feel better. After spending most of the time reading through the rest of Henry North's diaries, I wondered if an inability to compromise could be inherited. Henry certainly had his vision of the world and he didn't give a damn for anyone outside it.

After the Jewish holocaust went 1945-era viral, he jotted down the numbers from various camps, totalled them up, but made no comment. There was not even a suggestion of remorse for his part in that total. Sure, Canada might only have been able to save twenty thousand more than the pathetically few thousand it took in over a decade. It would still have been last, compared to other countries, but who knows how many potential Albert Einsteins, Ralph Laurens, or Marc Chagalls might have made our country greater?

Mom got back late from Montreal with masses of packages. She'd even bought a new piece of luggage to take her new clothes back to Toronto. She showed me one dress and, for a nano-second, I wondered if the sainted Henry had been worth the sacrifice. The dress was simply that great.

We took an early flight out next morning. It was only about twenty minutes in the air between Ottawa and Toronto but, what with security etc., it seemed like three hours before we finally saw Dad. While Mom introduced him to the Carruthers, I organized luggage carts and pulled the first pieces off the carousel. He had a limo waiting for us. We dropped Jo and her dad off at their hotel, stopped at Dad's office for a file he wanted and then headed for Dad's new house in a part of Toronto called Rosedale.

The streets were wide and the trees glorious in their scarlets, yellows and greens of fall. The houses were stately and old. Dad's house had seven bedrooms but I wouldn't have traded it for our Vancouver house. For one thing, Attila-ess was only four mansions away.

Mom said we'd have a hurried lunch and then hit the shops. Attila-ess, though, had other ideas. When I phoned to say hello, she commanded our attendance at "luncheon." Then Mom made the fatal mistake of telling her we only wanted a bite to eat because we needed to find a dress for me.

"In that case, we'll have soup and sandwiches," Attila-ess countered.

Attila-ess on my cherished shopping expedition? Mom sighed as she put the phone down. "Let's get it over with," she said simply. "Otherwise, you'll never find your dress. And, you never know. Maybe she'll change her mind."

Or break an ankle, I secretly hoped.

7

Attila-ess had everything ready, or rather the house-keeper did. The table was set beautifully, the silver polished. Everything was perfection—except the company. Mom looked normal but I could tell she was outraged that Attila-ess had muscled in on our plan to leave no shop standing.

To break the silence, I turned to Attila-ess. "Grand-mother," I said politely. "Do you know the Halders? They live around here."

Her back straightened immediately. "Not around here, child. Four, maybe five blocks over. Why? Do you know them?"

After I explained about Jas, and her strange lack of relatives, Grandmother frowned again. "They moved in years ago on a September 11. Everyone talked about it, wondering if it would be bad luck, and I think someone told me they had come from Vancouver. She did, at least."

I was excited. Helping Jas might wash away some of the scum I'd felt after reading Henry North's diaries. "Then, they might be her family."

Attila-ess frowned again. "Not likely. The Halders are Jews."

Mom said, as though it solved the problem, "Mrs. Green is a devout Anglican. It has to be a different family."

And with that we directed our energies to finishing the meal, but I couldn't stop wondering. Did Attila-ess have the same thoughts about Jews as Great-great grandfather? Religion seemed such a weird thing to know about a family you'd never met.

By the time we finished eating, the North car was at the door. After Attila-ess told the driver, "Simone's," I saw Mom's face tense up. She had probably three or four other shops in mind. No wonder she'd wanted to shop in Montreal. She must have been buying dresses for armor.

Simone's was a small shop and I don't know that I would have given it a second thought if I'd walked by it. But Attila-ess swept in trailing Mom and me in her wake. When a nervous shop assistant jumped to hold the door, I realized that Attila-ess was a prized customer.

Mom and I started prowling around, but Attila-ess took a seat on a chair—think armchair meets Chippendale—and waited. She'd look at me, then frown. After I while, it bugged me. But before I could ask, a wraith-like figure floated in from the back with a dress over her right arm.

Attila-ess stood. "Simone!"

"Mrs. North!"

They looked like football players as they did their genteel equivalents of chest thumps. Obviously, each thought the sun set on the other. I was truly amazed because I was sure that Simone didn't live in the TO land of milk and honey—Rosedale.

Simone drifted over to me and took my arm. "You must try this. It was made for you."

The next time Dr. Collins wanted an example of hyperbole, I would quote Simone.

I didn't know about the dress. It was blue—the exact color of my eyes, according to Simone. I still hadn't made my mind up when I put it on. I wore enough blue around school. Worse, the dress showed almost no cleavage. I had hoped for something a little more daring but, after I'd looked in the mirror, I realized that it made my teenage under-developed boobs look outstanding. Not Brazilian artificial, but great all the same.

When I walked out of the changing room and saw Mom's face, I knew that Simone had hit a home run. Mom, with her jaw dropped, and I stood there, while Simone and Attila-ess became action figures—imagining a tuck needed here, pulling the dress up to see different hemlines until they stilled and looked me over once again.

"It's perfect the way it is, Mrs. North," Simone asserted.

Attila-ess nodded her agreement. "Now, do you have a couple of other dresses for less formal occasions? The child will need something for Thanksgiving dinner, I imagine."

Before Mom could explode, I said, "I brought a dress from Vancouver."

Simone gave me a look that implied that Vancouver was in the middle of Antarctica before she glided away. As I turned for the change room, I heard Mom say, "Mother North, thank you for bringing us here. But I'm sure you're busy with thirty of us descending on you tomorrow. Jenn and I will finish up, browse for a while, and then find our own way home."

Attila-ess seemed deaf to everything Mom said. She

walked over to an aisle, plucked a dress off it, and handed it to me. "Try this on, Jenn."

It was a dullish-green, a color I'd never have thought of choosing in a million years but, as soon as I put it on, I began to respect Attila-ess. It was perfect. Comfortable and yet stylish enough that I could wear it to dinner at the fanciest restaurant. Or, more to the point, the North Thanksgiving dinner.

I'd always thought Grandmother looked so stylish because she had lots of money. Now I knew that wasn't true. Grandmother looked perfect because she had the most incredible dress sense. Mom was elegant but Grandmother had her beat. Mom's determination to shop in Montreal made more and more sense.

There was no need to go to other shops, at least for me. I walked out of Simone's with three perfect dresses. When I asked Mom if she wanted to browse the neighbourhood, she shook her head. But I had an idea. As we started going back towards Dad's, I leaned over to Grandmother. "Thanks for the dresses. For finding them, and for paying for them." I grinned when I added, "I was looking forward to emptying Dad's credit card."

Grandmother was obviously pleased to be thanked again. "It was my pleasure, Jenn. It's a shame that you live so far away. But maybe next year, you could go to Bishop Strachan or Havergal and we could do this more often."

Bishop Strachan? Not, if I had breath. That was the school with the silly collars and absurd initials—BS. And Havergal? I didn't know much about it, other than it wasn't in Vancouver. If I were honest though, I'd bet that the girls going to Strachan or Havergal probably thought that Prim Heights was a really stupid name for a school.

"I'm happy at Prim Heights," I told her. "Mom's family has its tradition there just as you Norths have yours here," I went on and felt stupid. Now I had both Mom and Attila-ess mad at me. Neutral ground. That's what I needed, so I leaned across again and asked, "Grandmother, can we go by the Halder house on the way home? When Jo comes tomorrow, she and I want to find out if they're connected to Jas."

I put my clothes away carefully in my bedroom in Dad's house then called out to see if he was home. To my absolute delight, Dan and Dave popped out of nowhere.

"Had to come down to Toronto to see our favourite sister," Dan told me, giving me a big kiss.

"Had to come down to Toronto for the Thanksgiving dinner," Dave corrected. "We had a command invitation."

"Doesn't matter," Dave went on. "How about you changing into something normal and we'll hit the lake?"

Mom heard the commotion and rushed into the room. "Why didn't someone tell me you were coming? How long can you stay?"

The twins looked at me, their eyes full of questions, when they saw the tearstains on Mom's face. "Only tonight," Dave told her. "We were just about to check out the waterfront with Jenn. Want to come along?"

Mom looked tempted. "There's dinner with your grandmother."

Dan puffed his chest out and beat on it. "I'm Superman. I'll ask her if we can have it an hour later. That'll give us more than enough time."

Mom fussed about while Dan went down the street to try his charms on Attila-ess. Dave let her pat imaginary lint from his sweater but he also looked across to me. The problem with Mom wasn't just in my head. The twins could see it as well.

While we waited, my phone did its drumroll. I picked up and it was Jo, wondering what I was doing. Then I had an amazingly brilliant thought. Her hotel overlooked Lake Ontario. "Hey," I said. "My brothers are here and we're just about to come downtown.

Why don't you and your dad meet us in the lobby of your hotel?" I looked at Mom who nodded okay.

It would be perfect. Mom and Mr. Carruthers could drink tea while the rest of us explored the area and talked about Mom's problem. But it didn't work out like that, even after Dan paired off with Jo. Dave was obsessed with his new girlfriend. Marielle hadn't seen the ocean, Marielle was beautiful. Marielle thought he was wonderful, and on and on. I thought I'd cry.

When we left, we arranged for Jo to come up to Dad's at ten the next morning by taxi. Together we would face the twin demons of the Halders and then the North Thanksgiving dinner.

Although Mom disapproved and made no bones about showing it, she sat Jo and me down the next morning and talked through strategies for us to use on the Halders. "Play the North card, Jenn," she began. "Most people here know of your grand-mother. She's not the type that hides her light behind a bushel."

That is one thing I give Attila-ess props for. She's out there, in your face and God help you if you get in her way. Mom also told us to make it absolutely clear that neither Jas nor Mrs. Green knew what we were doing.

We set out with a bit of a swagger because both of us knew we were doing a good deed. Jas wanted to find her family and we were trying to make that wish come true. But after three blocks, we looked at each other for reassurance. Were we right or were we busy-bodies, like Mom said? The closer we got, the more we wanted to turn around and go back to Dad's.

I swear we stood in front of the Halder's door for two minutes before Jo, with a do or die look on her face, rang the bell. It opened immediately and right away I knew we'd done the right thing. Mrs. Halder looked like Jas might in thirty years.

"I'm Jenn North," I started and felt embarrassed when I heard a sort of stutter. "My grandmother lives…"

Mrs. Halder smiled as she stopped me. "I know who Mrs. North is. Now, what are you collecting for?"

Jo and I looked at each other. Mom hadn't thought of this. "Nothing," I said quickly. "We're from Vancouver and just out here for Thanksgiving. But…"

Jo held out her hand. "I'm Jo Carruthers. We're sorry to bother you but one of our friends doesn't know anything about her relatives. Other than her mother of course." Jo stopped, as though amazed by her incoherence.

The discussion with Mom flashed through my mind. "Just tell them about Jas," she'd advised.

And so I began, "Jaslyn Green is a scholarship student at our school. She has a single mom who works two jobs to give Jas things like dance classes. Mrs. Green was a foster child, so Jas doesn't have any relatives on her mother's side and every time she tries to find out something about her dad, Mrs. Green freezes. Finally, because she has to know something about him for our project at school, Mrs. Green mentioned your name and address but said there was nothing but heartache here for Jas if she tried to find you."

Mrs. Halder's face changed as I spoke, going from a friendly smile, to frowns then nothing. A blank slate. A block of wood. No expression. Nothing. I knew I couldn't make things worse, so I rushed to finish, "We, that is, Jo and I, think you have to be related because Jas looks just like you."

Mrs. Halder turned away and ran down the hallway yelling "Mark" at the top of her voice. We heard a male voice answer, and then a door shut. We looked at the front door, and then each other. Did the open door mean we were to stay or go? Was Mrs. Green right? Was there nothing for Jas in Rosedale but heartbreak?

I pulled my phone out to ask Mom. Before she could answer, a man walked towards us, "I'm Mark Halder," he said and shook our hands. "Please come in."

He led us to a room with white puffy leather chairs, a huge television screen, lots of plants and glass tables. At the moment, photo albums littered them. Mrs. Halder, her face streaked with tears, had one in her hands.

She pointed to the photo of a man perched on top of a mountain peak. I recognized it immediately. It was called Mercy Street and was about an hour's drive north of Vancouver. He laughed as he looked at the camera and beside him, out of focus but still recognizable, was Mrs. Green. A pregnant Mrs. Green.

"That's Josh, my brother," Mrs. Halder said.

Josh wore scruffy jeans, a logger's red and black checked shirt, and a huge grin. His long black hair was a mass of riotous curls. He had a swimmer's long body and his resemblance to Mrs. Halder and Jas was unmistakable.

"Is that Jas's father?" Jo asked. She looked as stunned as I felt. Neither of us had expected the quest for Jas's relatives to be this easy.

"What happened?" I asked and pointed to the photo. "They look so happy."

"And just married happy," Mrs. Halder replied. "I only met her once. At dinner at my parents' place the night before this photo was taken. Josh had phoned to say he was bringing a friend but then he was terribly late. Mother held the meal back for at least an hour. We were half way through the main course when he eventually arrived and introduced us to Kate."

Mrs. Halder tidied up the albums, her face turned towards the table. It seemed an aeon before she looked up and continued, "Kate was obviously pregnant and that got our attention immediately. Then Josh said they were getting married the next morning, that he'd go to UBC rather than Stanford, and oh, by the way, did we want to come to their wedding."

She started crying. "Just like that. No lead in. No warning. Father went purple immediately."

I could imagine the scene. The lateness, the overcooked food, the shock of seeing a pregnant Mrs. Green. Mrs. Halder rocked back and forth a little as though the motion helped settle her. Finally she went on, the tears coming down like a torrent.

"You have to understand that Father had bragged all summer about Josh getting into Stanford's Business School. In fact, Josh was supposed to leave for California the following week. But after he explained that he had to go to UBC because that was the only way he could support himself and his new family, Father's temper erupted and all the ugliness of hell broke loose." Mrs. Halder didn't bother to mop up her tears and they ran unchecked down her face as she thought back to that terrible night. "After Father shouted 'Get an abortion' Josh went pale. He got up from the table, took Kate's hand, and that's the last time we saw him. He died the next afternoon. Just two hours after that photo was taken."

I dug my fingers into the white leather of my chair. My own tears poured down my face now. It was a horrible, tragic story. I cried for the young Mrs. Green. She must have been so upset and angry. I cried for the laughing Josh on the cliff, and for Jas whose life would have been so different if he'd lived. And then there was the father who'd destroyed his family with those three brutal words. How he must have wished he'd never said them.

"What about Mrs. Green?" Jo asked in a shaky voice. "Why didn't you help her or see if the baby needed anything?"

When Mrs. Halder broke into huge, ugly-sounding sobs, Mr. Halder produced a handkerchief and took her in his arms. Jo and I sat in increasing discomfort.

When she had quietened somewhat, Mr. Halder took over the explanation. "After Josh fell from the cliff, my in-laws blamed Kate. She'd wanted to go on the climb and had told everyone it would be her last until after her baby was born. People said Josh thought it would be too much for her but she'd talked him into it. Then, he was the one who fell." Mr. Halder held his hands out in the universal gesture of bewilderment.

"But…" Jo prompted.

"Kate sent a condolence card," Mrs. Halder said. "But Mother was too grief-stricken to want to have anything to do with it and she threw it into the fire. She wouldn't talk with Kate at the funeral. I think Kate reached out once more, asking if they'd like to know about the baby when it was born, but Mother was too bitter and Father still upset about everything to answer her."

And I thought my family situation was bad? Jas's was unimaginable. There was more to tell though and Mrs. Halder resumed the story.

"When they came to their senses and tried to find Kate a couple of months later, it was too late. She had disappeared. Josh had introduced her as Kate, so we didn't know her last name. Their friends said they only knew her as Kate something or other. A long European name like Rzepczynski. Almost every person said it differently and no one knew where she lived."

I frowned. It seemed way too casual, and I wondered if Kate had put the word out that she didn't want to be found by Josh's parents.

"What's more," Mrs. Halder continued, "we didn't know where or how they met. Josh had been fire-spotting in northern Alberta that summer, so we thought she must have lived there. Father hired private detectives but they turned up nothing."

I bet she was in Vancouver all along. Hiding in plain sight. It must have been horrible for her. She didn't have a family to fall back on. Who would have supported her? The rock climbers she'd been with? I was about to ask about Jas's grandparents when my phone pinged.

I looked at my watch and just about died. Talk about turning up late for meals! We should have been at Grandmother's for her big dinner. I got up and started to say my goodbyes, almost pushing Jo out of the room.

"What's the problem?" Mr. Halder asked.

"We're late for Thanksgiving dinner. At my grandmother's. We've got to go."

As we walked out the front door, I felt cheated. I wanted to know more. The Halders looked dumbstruck, as though a bit of their promised land had suddenly been snatched away from them. "When can you come back?" Mrs. Halder asked.

It was a good question. We were catching an early flight the next morning. Mr. Halder got his car from the garage and said he'd drive us to Grandmother's. On the way, I gave them Mom's phone number.

Mrs. Halder put it into her phone but still seemed distraught. "You've made us so happy. Now we know who Josh's baby is. The next step though is frightening. How do we get to know her? Can Kate forgive us and let us become part of her family?"

8

That, of course, was the billion dollar question.

But one I couldn't think about for several hours. Jo and I hadn't delayed the meal. It wouldn't be on the table for another couple of hours. But Grandmother had said midday and Mom still looked daggers at me when we arrived five minutes late. Late for nothing, but nevertheless late. Even Mr. Carruthers seemed disapproving.

Maybe he looked that way because Dad had him cornered. That was so typical. Dad hadn't worried about me. We hadn't even had breakfast together. Somehow, though, he'd sensed that Mom and Mr. Carruthers had become friends and he wanted to make sure Mr. Carruthers knew that Mom belonged to him. At least, knowing Dad and judging from his posture, that was probably what was going on.

Attila-ess told us to go into another wing of the house and join the other "youth." I don't like being called a youth. It rhymes with uncouth and makes me feel that way. I mumbled this to Jo, and then we braved the lion's den.

In that moment, I wished for one nano-second that I was Jas with absolutely no known relatives. There had to be about fifteen North youth, all looking at us with varying degrees of welcome. I was so glad Grandmother had chosen my dress because it easily outclassed those worn by my snotty female cousins. The guys were in suits and ties.

It was twelve o'clock in the afternoon and we looked like we were at a junior prom.

One of the male cousins looked halfway interesting. All the others wore subdued ties, but his had yellow swirls and looked like Van Gogh had painted it. He asked Jo if she'd like to see some of Grandmother's treasured family relics and Jo came back five minutes later with red cheeks and a stormy look in her eyes.

"Don't go anywhere with that creep," she announced to the girl cousins around me. "He can't keep his hands to himself. I told him if he touched me again, he wouldn't know what hit him."

"That's just Cecil," one of my cousins, Amanda, I

think, muttered. "You can't stop him. He's always like that."

Jo subsided into a chair and I knew she didn't agree. I introduced her to as many cousins as I could. It was unexpectedly difficult because I'd only heard of some of them. They all knew us, though. Cousin Belle asked when I was transferring out to Toronto and intimated that I'd only get into a "good" school if Grandmother arranged it. I bit my thumb at her and didn't answer back.

After that there was a general debate about schools. To my surprise, there was no preferred "North" school. Cecil, it turned out, went to Upper Canada College. "That's why he thinks he can do anything," Amanda grumbled. "All those guys think they're gods."

"Or will be," another cousin agreed.

Listening to them talk, I thought of St. Nick's, and of the difference there seemed to be between west and east coasts. Mom certainly wasn't thriving in Toronto but would Grandmother be able to function in Vancouver where nobody knew or cared about the great white Norths? I was caught up in my thoughts until a bell interrupted them. Time for chow—if I could use that word for Grandmother's dignified repast.

The surge of cousins was like a tsunami. Relentless. That is, until a male hand groped my bottom. Without thinking, I swung round and delivered my best backhand to Cecil's face.

"Bitch," he said angrily and grabbed his eye.

Everyone stopped dead in the narrow hallway, except for Jo who pushed through to stand beside me. "I warned you, creep," she said. "Keep your hands to yourself."

Amanda crept out of the mass of cousins as well. "That goes for all of us."

The meal, which should have been the highlight of the day, was anti-climatic. Amanda stuck with me and I discovered that I liked her. Not best friend territory, but enough to call her Mandy. Jo, though, had been collared by Grandmother. They sat on the opposite side of the room looking like bosom buddies, as they used to say.

Unbelievable.

Dad and Mom sat together, giving the appearance of a couple. Mom's elbows were tucked to her side in a way they probably hadn't been since finishing school. Dad gave her those "That's nice, dear" smiles a couple of times and I wondered who they were fooling. My stomach roiled with pain and I couldn't eat any more.

Home used to be where Mom and Dad were. Now I longed for Leith House at Prim Heights. It was safe, and I couldn't imagine that it would break what was left of my heart.

Everyone hung around after the meal for a while. Some seemed to be in genuine conversations—like Attila-ess and Jo, and Uncle Gerald and Mr. Carruthers. Much to my relief, Mom and Dad were among the first to leave. We said our good-byes and, as I was going out the door, I looked back.

My grandmother winked at me!

I stared. A wink from Grandmother? Then I heard her call across the room for Cecil and his father. I felt like giving her a standing ovation but, as I was already standing, that was impossible. So, I winked back.

The plan had been for Jo and me to leave for the airport early in the morning for the 7:30 flight. But Mr. Halder phoned Mom shortly after we'd arrived back at Dad's, and they talked for a long time. Then Mom phoned Mr. Carruthers and they'd talked long as well. The upshot of it all was a massive change in plans.

The Halders would have a late breakfast/early lunch with us at Jo's hotel downtown and we'd catch the 4:00 plane. Leith House and Mrs. Green knew of the new plans. Best of all, coach class had been full on the plan so someone had sprung for business. Life was good.

After the flight attendant finished fussing around us and the seat belt sign went out, Jo came across and settled into a tiny part of my compartment. After she got herself comfortable, she opened the conversation and my mouth gaped wide open when she said, "I like your grandmother. She's got attitude to spare. She loves you, you know."

No, I didn't know.

The captain broke in to say we'd reached cruising altitude and all that stuff, and after he'd wound down I said, "Well, what about Mom? She and Grandmother are always fighting."

"Of course they are," Jo answered. "Think about it. They're fighting over the same man and his children. Your grandmother desperately wants to get to know you but she lives in Toronto. So even though she knows it will cost her in the end, she manipulates. Your mom's a strong woman and can't stand it. That's why everything's a mess. But, love, strange as it sounds, is at the bottom of it all."

I glared at Jo, but she smiled like her life's ambition was to destroy my assumptions. Once I thought about it, she kind of made sense. Grandmother, like a broody hen, wanted all her chicks about her. Mom's traditions and roots—unlike those of anyone else in the North family—were west coast. Maybe if we lived closer, I'd never call Grandmother Attila-ess.

Jo and I checked the screen for movie choices but nothing appealed. Both of us wanted to talk about the bombshells the Halders had dropped at lunch. Jas was rich. Filthy rich. Spoiled trust fund child rich.

Few people have heard of the Vancouver Dicksons but everyone knows the Adele Trust. It's a holding company, an investment conglomerate worth billions of dollars. Most importantly, it's owned by Nathaniel Dickson and Jas's dad was Josh Dickson. Jas has had a trust fund ever since she was born but no one knew how to find her.

Now, however, she *was* found.

The Dicksons wanted to know her. Mr. Halder said they told him they had fourteen years to catch up on. They'd do anything to help Mrs. Green forgive them. How to get that done was the real question.

We were still trying to think of ways to tell Jas—because everyone agreed that it would be best if she told Mrs. Green—when the plane swooped over the mountains, and the lights of Vancouver twinkled up at us.

Ironically, Mrs. Green was the first person we saw

after we'd collected our baggage. It hurt to smile at her like everything was normal. She asked after Mom and Dad and didn't seem surprised when I shrugged and said they were fine.

All of us knew I was lying.

After school the next day, Jas insisted on walking back to Leith House with us. She wanted to see the finery we'd bought. On the way, we told her we'd met the Halders.

She stopped walking immediately and kicked some leaves someone had carefully raked into a mound. "Oh my word. What on earth will Mom say?"

Jo kept walking and Jas had to run a little to catch up. "It's not like we went behind anyone's back," Jo told Jas. "Your mom gave you the clues. Jenn and I just followed up."

Jas stopped again. She looked at the ground when she asked, "What are they like?"

I grabbed her arm. I'd had enough of the stop and start routine. "Come on, Jas. Let's get to Leith. One thing though, I liked your aunt and uncle. They have three kids. Two are married, and there's a twelve year old called Adele."

Jas shook herself free and stopped again. "That's weird. Adele's my middle name. Mom says that's what my father wanted."

"I'm not going to have this conversation on the street," Jo said, walking more quickly than ever. "Jenn and I aren't going to tell you another word until we get to the dorm."

But once we'd reached our bedroom, Jas wanted to see our dresses. Jo pulled hers out of the closet and Jas examined it like it was pure gold, slipping her hand under the protective plastic to gently touch the gossamer-like silk. She stepped back, looked at Jo, then back at the dress. "It's perfect," she said. "That shimmery gold? Perfect."

I took my dress out and Jas instantly came over. She blinked. "Where on earth did you find these? I can't believe that you found two dresses that are so perfect for you. The blue is wonderful, Jenn. It's the exact same color as your eyes and I love the cut of the bodice."

Jo and I looked at Jas in amazement. Who knew that a *fashionista* lurked under our school uniform? She was genuinely excited by our dresses. More than we were. I grinned as I imagined Grandmother taking Jas shopping. An instant sorority of two.

"What's your dress like?" I asked.

Brought back to earth, Jas's face clouded over. "It's a soft paprika red," she muttered.

"You'll look good in it," Jo told her.

"If it gets finished," she said so softly that I wasn't quite sure I heard her correctly.

Jo must have. "Is your mom making it?"

Jas looked angry. "It's so not fair. She got an extra job to buy the right shoes. I hate knowing that she's working so hard to give me a night of fun."

I hated it too. But Mrs. Green's hours of sacrifice were over. The problem was how to break the news.

"Starbucks," Jo said. "Give me a minute and I'll see if I can get village privileges."

That was one of the worst things about boarding. Unless we went with a Grade 11 or 12, most of the time we needed permission to go down the street for a cup of coffee. But I trusted Jo's charm and helped Jas tenderly put our dresses back in the closet.

Fifteen minutes later we hit Starbucks. After our double-double routine, Jas looked at us. "I have to be home by five, so hurry up. Tell me what this is all about."

"Don't worry. We'll hurry. We've got volleyball at five as well."

So taking turns, we told her about walking down the street to the Halders' house, about standing outside and wondering if we should actually knock on the door. Then how we almost fled when Mrs. Halder had run down the hall and how excited she became when she realized that Jas was her brother's long-lost child.

Jas examined her coffee mug as though her life depended on it and I was glad that Jo had thought of telling Jas at Starbucks . It was the right spot. Jas didn't have to react to us and there was no more stopping in the street. She could stare into her mug as she processed the amazing story. When Jo finished the lead-up story, I jumped right in.

"Jas, you've got grandparents right here in Vancouver," I told her. Her head jerked up in surprise and she began demolishing every paper napkin in sight. "Mom thinks they live in one of those mansions in The Crescent. We didn't give them a lot of details about you. They do know that you go to Prim Heights because we had to tell Mrs. Halder that. Everyone's agreed that the next step should be yours. Re family contact, that is."

Jas seemed overwhelmed. I didn't blame her because there was more to come. "Jas," Jo said, taking the plunge. "Your family is uber rich. Think about your middle name and put trust after it. That's who you are. Your grandparents are worth billions."

"The Adele Trust?" Light, and something like joy, flashed into Jas's eyes until anger replaced them. "Okay," she sneered. "if what you're saying is right, why does Mom have to get two jobs to send me to a dance?"

Jo and I looked at each other. "That's a long story and one that your Mom or the Dicksons should tell you. Not us," I told her. I didn't want to tell Jas that her grandfather had wanted her aborted. He could tell her. If he had the guts, that is. I, however, wasn't going near it.

"Plus there's one more amazing thing," Jo went on. "You're Jewish."

Jas almost knocked our coffee cups off the table. "No, I'm not," she exploded. "This is all lies. I'm Anglican."

"Anglican, because that was the way your great-grandfather got out of Austria when the Nazis came. Then, he had to say he was Anglican so that he could get into Canada because it was on his passport. But he left a lot of the family assets behind that the Nazis confiscated. They've just got some back. This century. More than sixty years after they were stolen though that's another long, incredible story. But Jas, your share is in a trust fund in Switzerland. Twenty-five million dollars."

Jas looked as though she didn't know whether to laugh or cry. "Right," she eventually said in a voice that oozed sarcasm. "I walk into some bank in Zurich.

I say that I'm Jaslyn Green and please may I have twenty-five million dollars? I don't believe it."

"You should," Jo said, as she gathered up our mugs.

Jas turned to me, as though I were the sane one. "Twenty-five million dollars?"

"It might be more. It's your father's share. Jas, it doesn't matter if you get along with your grandparents or not. If they died right now and you weren't in their wills, you'd still get that money." I looked at the clock on the wall and groaned. Why was there always time for boring things but never enough for exciting ones?

"Look, Jas, we all have to go. We've got a volleyball game, and there's the tennis dance on Friday. Let's talk Sunday after church. I don't want to huddle in corners at school and whisper everything. Is your Mom okay if we stay over on Saturday?"

"Is Mike coming on Sunday?"

That was one of the new things Mom had warned me about. St. Nick's, Mom and Mr. French had worked it out so that Mike came to church with us every second Sunday. He'd lunch with us or Mrs. French would drive him wherever he had to be. They said it would give him a sense of stability. I don't know if it did but it was sure great to catch up with him.

I didn't know what was going on in Jas's head the next day. I sensed a volcano, but all she'd talk about was the tennis dance. I couldn't complain. I'd set the terms. But her cheeks were flushed and her eyes had that overexcited look little kids get if they haven't had enough sleep. Jo tried to get her to talk once but Jas snapped her head off.

"Sunday. You said we'd talk Sunday, so Sunday it is."

Sunday sounded like the valley of doom. I think all of us put our hopes for fun in the tennis dance.

After it, who knew?

9

Coach Copeland got permission for us to skip our last classes on Friday and Mom made appointments for our hair, nails, etc. We wanted to ask Jas to go with us but didn't have the courage. I asked Mom about it when she phoned to let me know the arrangements. She said she'd hinted at giving Jas the mini-spa package as an early Christmas present but Mrs. Green told her they didn't accept charity.

Charity with the Dickson and Zurich money around the corner?

Kimberley Leung was livid when she found out we were skipping class to go to a spa. "It's not fair," she vented. But when was anything fair in her world? Then she took her spite into the unforgiveable. "I see Jas Green isn't going with you. What's the matter?

You didn't want her because her mom's your house-keeper?"

I wanted to pull her hair until she screamed for mercy but Jo stepped between us. "Chill, Kimberley. It's not like a spa's going to show up on our Cambridge acceptance emails," she told her.

"You won't be so smug when you see Kimberley's humanities presentation. Mrs. Leung hired a graphic designer," Patti Cheng contributed, trying to goad us into retaliation.

A graphics designer for a Grade 9 project? I admit going to the Archives was a bit much. But with Jo's father in Ottawa, it had seemed natural at the time. Plus, Jo couldn't have found out the stuff about her great-grandfather until late November if she had ordered it on line and she would never have understood the story because of the abbreviations. Still, a graphics designer seemed over the top. Hadn't Mrs. Leung ever learned that less is more sometimes?

As it turned out, Dr. Collins retaliated for us in a way I'd never imagined. Dear Cathy leave-it-to-the-last-moment Semple had got herself kicked out of her group. Supposedly she had been working on refugee children — the exact same topic Kimberley slaved over. Dr. Collins's eyes had an amused look when she said, "Kimberley, I'm sure your group is further ahead than anyone else's. Cathy can fit in with you and won't hold you back. Just make sure she does her own work though, will you?"

I laughed and had to cough to cover it up. The look on Kimberley's face was priceless. If she had been even one percent nicer, I would have felt sorry for her. But after what she said about Jas? Never.

At first, all the arrangements for the dance seemed perfect. The limo picked us up at Leith and then purred its way to my place for Jas. Our dates looked perfect in their tuxes. Blake, Jo's date, was a tiny bit shorter than her and had a wicked sense of humour. "I'm supposed to charm you into playing tennis," he started out. "But I'm not supposed to mention the word or put pressure of any kind on you," he said, in a perfect parody of Coach Copeland's voice.

I sort of knew Jim, my date. His brother hung out with Dave and Dan so I'd met him a few times. Nice, but not enough to give me a fluttery feeling in my stomach. Neither he nor Axel, Jas's date, played tennis. They'd simply been recruited as pretty faces and good dancers to make sure we had a good time. Jim said he'd only got the gig because he knew me. Axel went to the door to get Jas and we laughed when Blake remarked that Ms. Copeland had missed her time. Coach would have made an outstanding World War II general.

"Maybe, she's been and done it—the general thing, that is. I've often thought she's a reincarnation of the queen of the Amazons," Jo said with a smile.

We were still laughing and making ridiculous jokes when the limo arrived at the golf club. To our surprise we were split up. It turned out that the head table needed Blake and Jo's presence. We were herded off to a side table. I was still smiling at something Jim said about Coach not appreciating his importance when I saw the two adults at our table. I'd never met Nathaniel or Evelyn Dickson but I'd seen them at Dad's golf club and knew who they were. What a way for Jas to meet her grandparents.

Suddenly I was blazingly angry. Jas loved dancing. Of the three of us, she was the one who had looked forward to this dance the most. She was also the one with her mind and emotions in absolute turmoil. With incredibly bad manners, I pushed my way forward almost knocking Jas down in the process. "I hope you remember me, Mr. Richards," I said, glaring at him and trying to make sure he went along with the wrong name thing. "And you, Mrs. Richards. I'm Jenn North. This is my friend, Jaslyn Green, and our dates Jim Ferguson and Axel Mannering."

Mr. Dickson hadn't earned his billions by being stupid. With incredible smoothness, he smiled and asked us about our schools. His questions brought Jas to life. Her answering smile was wide and her dark hair shone. She looked completely relaxed and when Axel asked her to dance she accepted eagerly. Jim asked me as well. I stood and looked at the Dicksons. "I had to call you Mr. and Mrs. Richards. Part of her is furious about the little she knows and Mrs. Green hasn't been told anything. We'll probably tell her on Sunday. If we get the courage."

"We're grateful, Jennifer. For everything. She has a great friend in you."

I blushed. Truth to tell, I was dreading Saturday and Sunday.

"What was that about?" Jim asked, as he led me away.

I knew I could trust him so I told him that the Dicksons were Jas's grandparents and that there had been a huge row between them and Mrs. Green. "They've never met, and it would have spoilt tonight if she knew who they were."

Jim shuddered. "Thanks Jenn. You've saved me from a fate worse than something-or-other. Girls crying their eyes out would have shredded my reputation." He squared his shoulders and threw out his chest. "Me? I'm the number one ladies' man. Just ask your coach."

I laughed as I told Jo about it later that night. "He's cute," she said.

"He's my brothers' friend's brother."

"But still cute."

I nodded. "The Dicksons were nice. I actually liked them. They had so obviously muscled in on the dance. It must have cost them big time, fifty thou at least, to get Jas and me at their table. But having done that, they let Jas come to them. She had a great time and Axel's already asked her to St. Nick's Halloween dance."

"It's a good job he asked early. She won't be in his league by then," Jo muttered cynically as she put out the light.

I lay awake for a while. Axel and Jas had been such great dancers that they'd had the floor to themselves a couple of times. Jas had been so alive as she laughed with him and been too caught up in the joy of dancing to notice her grandparents' intense interest. In the breaks she'd talked to them almost as naturally as she did with Mom.

As I fell asleep, I couldn't help dreading Sunday. I had the profound conviction that telling Mrs. Green would be my job. What on earth would she say when she found out?

Sunday brunch was brutal. Not the food, of course. It was great. As no one had small talk, we ate in silence. Even Mrs. Green sensed that as soon as we put the dishes in the washer, something would happen.

Or not. Some kind of defense mechanism kicked in and I slipped into hostess mode and offered capps, lattes, or tea. Whatever. Anything to defuse the tension. I saw Jo raise an eyebrow and realized that I'd upstaged Mrs. Green. She was the hostess, not me. Oops. Messy oops.

Mrs. Green showed her maturity immediately though, and said, "That would be fine, Jenn." Then, after I'd served everyone, she got straight to the point. "Now, you three. You've obviously got something to tell me. Please don't say that Axel's gay."

She wasn't being funny. Axel had come over yesterday with a bunch of late dahlias from his mother's garden and taken Jas for a walk. Mrs. Green liked him. Jas wouldn't talk about him and I felt wildly envious.

Mrs. Green continued, "Now which one of you is going to talk? Jenn?"

I was still under the firm conviction that Jas was the

one who should do the talking but she stared at the floor and muttered, "Tell Mom what you told me."

Jo nodded. "I'll start." She looked at Mrs. Green. "When you gave us that clue about Jas's relatives in Toronto, we followed it up because the Halders live only a few blocks from Jenn's grandmother." She gulped, seemed to gather her courage and went on, "Mrs. Halder looks so much like Jas and she cried and cried when we told her that." Then she ratted and didn't dare look at me when she finished with, "Jenn can tell you the rest."

Thanks, I said under my breath. "Mrs. Halder showed us pictures of her brother, Josh," I began and looked across at the apprehensive-looking Mrs. Green. "The one I liked best was taken two hours before he fell off a cliff. It had you standing beside him."

Mrs. Green's eyes widened until they almost reached her ears. She knew what was coming next and feared it.

But I was not going near the fight at the Dickson's dinner table or Mr. Dickson's outrage. They could sort that out themselves. I took another deep breath and looked across the table at Mrs. Green. "Mrs. Halder said they searched everywhere for you. Once they got over the shock of Josh's death, that is. She said they didn't know your last name. For some reason, they thought it was one of those long, hard to pronounce European ones and that you came from Alberta. That's where they searched."

Jas was pleating the white tablecloth with nervous fingers. Without looking up, she asked, "Where were you, Mom?"

"Out in Cloverdale. One of my friends let me stay in her basement."

Cloverdale was full of young families trying to get ahead. Mrs. Green would have fitted right in. It was only about forty-five minutes from the center of Vancouver but it might have been in Newfoundland. That's how far it was from the world of Mr. and Mrs. Dickson.

Jas wasn't finished. In her place I'd have a million questions and I wondered what she'd ask next. I didn't have to wait long. She flicked a fast glance at her mother and went back to pleating the tablecloth. "Why didn't you go to them? The Dicksons? You wouldn't have had to work so hard. Jenn says I have a trust fund."

This was news to Mrs. Green. She turned to me. "What's she talking about?"

"Actually, she has two. One in Switzerland and one

here that belonged to Josh," I told her. "Didn't you know?"

She frowned, obviously trying to remember. "He said he had money but not enough for Stanford and the baby's medical expenses unless he stayed in Canada. That's why he was enrolling at UBC. I didn't know he had a trust fund. I thought he was talking about a savings account." She poured herself another cup of tea as if she wanted to settle her nerves. She shook her head, "And all this time there was a trust fund? Tell me about it."

"Josh's father set aside money for his children once his business started doing really well."

"Really well" was the understatement of the year! Going stratospherically viral was more like it. I choked off a giggle. Jo glared at me and continued the story, "Because the Dicksons knew a baby probably existed, they didn't collapse Josh's fund. Whatever was in it has been collecting interest all this time, waiting for his heir to show up. That was the Dicksons' way of keeping faith with Josh. They said it was their repentance. It will pay for whatever schools Jas wants to go to and there's an allowance as well. After Jas turns thirty, she gets the whole thing and can do whatever she wants with it. Her dad had to wait till he was thirty, as well. That's probably why he didn't tell you about it. He wouldn't be able to use it for years."

I didn't know how well I'd process as much information at this but Jas glommed onto one thing. "I can pay my own way at Prim Heights? I won't have to be a scholarship kid anymore?"

"Exactly. But, there's more," I said. "Much more."

"More money, more information," Jo confirmed. "Tell them, Jenn. Get to the fun part."

I tried to sort out which part of the story she meant. As Jo said, there was more information—about the Dicksons, the Zurich money, and Jas's roots. Looking across the table to Jas who was now trying to smooth out her pleats, I said, "Jas, most of the worst is over. Believe it or not, you've already met your grandparents."

Mrs. Green glared at me, "She has? No one asked my permission."

"They didn't ask mine either," I retorted, wishing for a fleeting second that I'd never gone near the Halders. "They were at the tennis dance, Jas. I introduced you to them as the Richards because I didn't want anything to spoil that night. But their real name is Dickson, and they live on The Crescent."

Huge, hundred year old mansions lined The Crescent. Jas looked across at Mrs. Green, "Is this right?"

Mrs. Green nodded slowly. "If they haven't moved, she's right. I met them there the one time your father took me."

Jas resumed her furious pleating as though she knew there was a lot she wasn't being told. She looked up at me for several seconds, "Do you swear that you didn't know they'd be at our table?"

"Absolutely," I said without taking a breath. I put my right hand up like I'd seen pictures of people doing in court when they were swearing an oath. "Jas, you've got to believe me. I would not have taken a single chance on ruining that dance. Not when we had gorgeous dresses and such hot guys."

"I can vouch for that," Jo said. "When Jenn told me your grandparents were at her table, I couldn't believe it and I was angry too."

Jas nodded. "Thanks." She looked at her mother, "Mom, I liked them. I wouldn't have if I'd known who they were. I wouldn't have said a word to them. But they seemed kind and interested in everything. I told them all kinds of things." She shook her head. "Mom, I had no idea who they were. I swore I wasn't going to meet them, until they'd talked to you. You've got to believe me."

Mrs. Green's eyes were teary. While the afternoon was hard on all of us, I suspect it was hardest for her.

She still must be wondering exactly how much of her story Jo and I knew. But she reached out to Jas and in a second they were hugging each other. "It's all right, Jas. I get it. But you've got to understand one thing, though. When the Dicksons decide they want something, they usually get it."

I hoped for her sake that the Dicksons decided they wanted forgiveness and were prepared to go down on their knees for it if necessary.

Jo suddenly pushed her chair back and got up. "Jenn, we need to get back to school. You don't know it, but we have a date with a tennis court."

10

When we got to the courts, Coach Copeland stood at the gate bouncing her racquet off one of her knees. "You're late," she greeted us.

"On time," Jo said, beginning to stretch.

"You'll be late after you change."

Change into what? Jo and I already had reasonably decent shorts and tees on. Not Wimbledon white, I must say, but decent.

Obviously Coach Copeland didn't agree. "Tennis court, tennis gear. To be a winner, you have to start from the outside. That means you wear the clothing appropriate for a champion."

I wondered when Coach had last seen Flirty.

Jo, however, kept her cool. "Winning's inside out, Coach. You can teach us everything possible, skill-wise, but if we haven't got the heart to win, we won't. That's my advantage over Flirty. I know I can beat her. She only thinks she can beat me."

Coach must not have taken debate at university. She passed on the chance to wax philosophical about Jo's viewpoint and pointed to the court instead, "Get started. Rally to begin with."

As I walked past her to get onto the court, I thanked her for the trouble she'd gone to for Jas and me, telling her we'd had a marvelous time. But things had obviously changed since Friday night. "We have to concentrate on your backhand, Jennifer. Jo's forehand is too good to waste playing that side of the court." As I walked on to the court, she shouted across to Jo, "After you're warm, give her three to nine."

I had no idea what the three to nine meant, but I understood what was not being said. The spider had spun her web and I was now trapped. I shuddered, briefly wondering if it had been worth it. Jim hadn't been that great as a date. Nice, and even fun, but my heart hadn't throbbed. Jas had got flowers; neither Jo nor I got anything.

Except Coach Copeland's undivided attention.

But I didn't mind rallying with Jo. She didn't try to embarrass me but she made me work. After a while, we had a peaceful rhythm. Three forehands, run across court, nine shots to my backhand, run across court. And so on.

Coach, though, didn't want us to get settled. "Practice your serves, girls," she called, and Jo immediately blasted something past me. And that was precisely why Coach was so interested in my backhand and why she had given up a Sunday afternoon to run a private practice session for us.

Jo's serve was pro-quality and Jo refused to play with anyone other than me. I didn't know whether to be proud or cry.

The dance was a turning point in our lives. We didn't see much of Jas after it and had no way of finding out how things were with the Dicksons. Not that it was our business of course. But both of us prayed that things would work out. Volleyball switched into high gear. We played league during the week and tournaments every weekend.

It was a good thing that neither Blake nor Jim had followed up. We literally had no time for them.

Therefore it goes without saying that Jo and I were dumbstruck when Jas showed up at one of our practices and our coach introduced her as our new scorer. She'd go to our remaining games, including tournaments. I had no idea what to make of it. Jas scurried home as soon as we went to the change rooms so there was no chance to talk. Volleyball had even put our term project on the backburner. Or so I thought.

Truth to tell, I wasn't much interested in it any more. My story wasn't worth telling. When it all came down to it, who cared that the sainted Henry was an anti-Jewish bigot?

I did, of course. It made me bone-deep sad and so ashamed I didn't know how to live with it.

I kept turning facts over in my mind, trying to understand him. I was no further ahead when Dr. Collins put a calendar up in the classroom and asked us to sign up for the days we wanted to give our presentations on. Oh my. The leather had hit the road and the proverbial you-know-what had hit the fan. Whatever expression I used, doomsday was coming.

Kimberley Leung always sat center front. Of course. No one could imagine her anywhere else. Anywhere else would have been unfair. She raced to the calendar and immediately blocked out the last three dates. Her work was already finished but wanted to see her opposition in case her mom needed to hire Mark Zuckerberg to give her project the extra zumpp.

Jo and I sat in the back of the room with Jas a row in front. We signaled her to sign us up but we could tell by the time she got there that the calendar was full. Except for the first three days which meant we'd lead off in two weeks. But that was also the same time that our volleyball team would play for the city championship.

Dr. Collins looked at us and smiled. "Well, shall I write the 3Js here for all three days?"

I did the math again and my head screamed conflict. We mightn't even be in school during those days. I put my hand up and explained the problem. Dr. Collins looked back at her calendar. "I had planned to do some testing here," she said, pointing to a space in the following week that had been blocked out. "Suppose I switch the dates?"

I nodded but Jas's hand shot up like a rocket. "That wouldn't work either, Dr. Collins. The team's been invited to one last tournament. We'll be out of class then as well."

Kimberley Leung turned and gave me her "It's not fair" glare and I was tempted to ask Dr. Collins if she'd give us Kimberley's dates. Volleyball had to be finished by then.

Dr. Collins looked frustrated as well when she turned to us. "How long will your presentation be? Two classes or three?"

"Three," Jo said without a moment's pause. "But we're not interconnected. I'm almost done, so I could go there," she went on, pointing to the first date on the calendar. "Jas and Jenn could fit in after that on spare days. Would that work?"

"You understand that it's still a group mark?" Dr. Collins asked.

We nodded. Jo was absolutely right. We didn't have to go one after the other. We could fit in whenever Dr. Collins said, providing I was last. I still had no idea how to present Great-great grandfather.

After class finished, Jo and I caught up with Jas just as she was leaving the room. "What were you talking about? Another tournament?" I asked.

Jas looked very smug, very sure of herself. "It's an inter-provincial one. We have to fly to it." Her voice had a note in it that made me suspect she was looking forward to the flying part. I knew she'd flown at least once, the time her mother took her to Disneyworld. Maybe she hadn't flown since then.

Her smile was wide as she went on, "Coach hasn't said anything because she's been waiting for the funding to come through. We're getting a new sister school and this is the first official visit. It's only been confirmed this morning."

I felt sick. The sister school thing hadn't set off the weird feeling in my stomach. Prim Heights was always getting sister schools. But the word "funding" made my stomach queasy. Think bungee cord queasy.

I knew two ultra-rich people, two ultra-rich very determined people—one male, and one female.

"The sister school wouldn't be in Toronto, would it?" I asked Jas, as sweetly as possible.

The next few days went by in a blur. Whatever time was left after school and volleyball was snapped up by Coach Copeland.

She had an insatiable appetite for work on my backhand. One day she showed us the list of tournaments she'd entered us in after Christmas. When they were over, I'd have enough frequent flyer points to go anywhere I'd wanted.

Like Tahiti.

Fortunately that was a free block. "Don't book anything in those dates," I told Coach, pointing to the calendar. "I'm going away with my mother."

Coach shrugged. "No problem. Jo can play with Susannah."

Susannah, otherwise known as Flirty.

"Jo's going away with her father those weeks, as well," Jo announced, having walked in at the right moment.

As Coach and Jo entered into a prolonged discussion, I looked at the long list of tennis matches and sighed. All this because we'd wanted Jas to go to a dance? I don't know if cheated was the right word or not but I definitely felt ground down. What was in it for me?

To make matters impossibly worse, Jo fell in love. Caleb was one of Axel's friends and super-tall. I was happy for Jo about that. She'd be able to wear heels. Caleb was a star rugby player. If you haven't seen rugby, there's something called a lineout. It's rugby's equivalent to a jump ball in basketball. Anyway that was Caleb's thing, plus being hot, hot, hot.

That's really all I knew about Caleb. Jo went all gooey-eyed when his name was mentioned. As Mom would say, it sucked drier than the Sahara when Kimberley, of all people, told me that Caleb and Jo, Axel and Jas had a double date planned for Saturday night.

I finally got Kimberley. It was SO unfair.

When I told Mom, she understood but told me to get over it. Life was often unfair.

Leith House had all kinds of things for us boarders to do on Saturday nights. I'd never bothered with them, because we usually went home. Now, Jo would be staying there Saturday night, and I'd be alone in the dorm. Of course, I could have gone home as well, but spending Saturday with Mrs. Green was not an attractive option. I had nothing against Mrs. Green of course, but it would have been awkward.

Kimberley and Mom were right. The world was unfair.

I studied Saturday's list of activities but nothing appealed. I could spend time working on the sainted Henry but the problem was that I already knew too much. I didn't understand him and more research wouldn't help that.

I gave in, threw myself on the bed and cried. Loneliness was a new thing. There had always been Mom or the twins before if things hit rock bottom. After a while, I got a grip on myself. I'd do what no one expected.

I booked a tennis court and put one of the ball machines to work on my "appalling" backhand. I hit each ball savagely and refused to think of Jas and Jo at the movies. I'd hear enough about their date after church when Jo unveiled her great-grandfather's story and we'd put her presentation together.

Soon I was swearing under my breath at the machine's relentlessness. Whether I was ready or not, it sent ball after ball. Eventually it ran out and only when I went to refill it, did I notice who was practicing next to me.

Blake. Jo's date from the dance. He'd booked the other machine. "What are you doing here?"

He jogged across. "Special dispensation. Our machines are being serviced in the far reaches of the universe. Anyway, we don't have them, so Coach Copeland me offered yours for tonight. I think it's a quid pro quo leftover from the dance."

That made a weird sort of sense. St. Nick's had given her those extra two tickets. Obviously, there had to be some kind of payback. I'd only ever thought about what those tickets had meant for me. Now I wondered what they might have cost the school.

Blake laughed at the look on my face. "Don't feel guilty. Your machines are better than ours. Besides, I didn't think you'd ever notice me," he grinned and went on. "I've been making the most amazing shots, thinking I'd get a standing O. But no. Nothing. Nada. Zero. I'm heartbroken and unnerved. I bet la Copeland loves your total concentration."

"Hah. She thinks I'm a pain in her royal behind."

I felt the first flutterings of happiness when he said, "She does? She must have pink and purple blinders on. But if you're such a pain, why are you on the team?"

I laughed. "Long, long story."

He didn't miss a beat. "And one I want to hear. You're a boarder, aren't you? When's your curfew?"

Happiness stirred again. "Eleven o'clock."

He looked at his watch. "How about this? We each put one more bucket of balls in the machines, slog away till they're finished, and then go to Starbucks. You can tell me this long, long story there. What do you say?"

Village privileges?

Out of bounds on a Saturday night?

Expulsion?

In one short two-second span, I gave myself every reason not to go.

"Great," I said instead.

11

I think I got away with breaking the rules because no one expected Ms. Jennifer Anne North of Primrose Heights to break them. Truth to tell, neither had I. And neither had Mom, when I phoned her the next morning before leaving for church.

"Once is fine, Jenn. Don't make it a habit," she said. Then after a second or two, she asked, "What's he like, this Blake?"

"He's in grade eleven, on St. Nick's tennis team, and his parents live near the Dicksons."

"So, he's respectable. I'm not particularly worried about his family or St. Nick's," Mom told me. "What's he really like?"

"He's kind, funny, and on the rebound. He needed someone to talk to as much as I did. He said he'd like to see me again but when we tried to set a time, he's as tightly scheduled as I am. We've made a tentative coffee date at Starbucks for Tuesday providing I can get village privileges."

"Make Blake understand that you can't break rules to see him," Mom responded in her Mom-must-be-obeyed voice.

I promised that I wouldn't be the first Jennifer Anne to get expelled from Prim Heights. I felt better after talking with Mom but, although I hurried, I was late for church. Mike smirked at me so I glared back, and there went all my good resolutions.

After she had taken Mike to his rugby game, Mrs. Green fussed. "Are you all right, Jenn? It's not like you to be late for anything, especially church."

If only she knew that a new Jenn was emerging. A Jenn that didn't mind breaking a few rules here or there or even being late for church. Jenn Goody-Two-Shoes was gone forever. After all, what did I have to live up to? The sainted Henry?

Lunch was sort of brittle. Jas and Jo sensed that I had little interest in their date although I politely asked about it. Mrs. Green looked at me occasionally and seemed perplexed. It was a relief to go down to the basement to talk about our project. But before we could begin, Jas told us why she was so excited by the

Toronto trip. Mrs. Green was going as a chaperone. She and Jas would stay at Grandmother's.

I hadn't time to catch my breath before she said that the Dicksons were going as well. Mom had suggested our Toronto games as neutral territory. Apparently if they watched the games and cheered for us, the ice might be broken. I hoped Mom was right. Jas and I would have to give our presentations a few days after we got back and we didn't need the Dickson problem to escalate. Jas had almost no idea what her story would be. If she couldn't talk with her grandparents, I didn't know what she'd do.

I didn't have to worry about Jo however. She was ready for her "reveal." She asked us to give her five minutes then reappeared, dressed entirely in black. "This is my great-grandfather Bill's story," she announced.

After she finished telling it both Jas and I were grabbing Kleenexes out of the box like there was no tomorrow. Then we sat down and worked out how to present it. While Jo told the story, I'd provide visuals and Jas would look after the sound. We had three days to get it done.

Jas and I worked furiously and, although we got together a couple of times to get synchronized, she didn't share anything about her mom or the Dicksons. I desperately hoped and prayed there'd be some kind of resolution. Not just for Jas's sake. I was being selfish. Tahiti depended on it.

Three days later, Jas and I plugged our computers into the Smartboard. Dr. Collins settled the class down, and then Jo walked in dressed in black pants and turtleneck. She handed the written part of her presentation to Dr. Collins who sat back with a smile on her face. The class leaned forward. For once, the last class of the day looked interesting.

I flashed pictures of a 1930s rugby game in Vancouver onto the smart board and a joyous riff of ragtime echoed through the speakers for about twenty seconds. There was absolute quiet when Jo began, "This is the story of my great-grandfather, William Carstarphan Stewart, and of his war. After Bill's father was killed at the Battle of the Somme in 1915, his mother got as far away from Europe as possible. She settled in West Vancouver, in a house that nestled against Lighthouse Park and there she grieved.

"Bill was popular in school and played rugby. In fact, that's how he met Babs, the woman he'd marry. At a rugby match. He ran after a ball at Brockton Oval, couldn't stop, and crashed in her picnic basket. He broke his leg and she came to see him in hospital. They talked, got to know each other, and when he proposed he told her that she was his east and west, his moonlight on a tranquil sea. At least, that's the family legend.

"After marriage, Bill became an undercover cop for the Vancouver Police. Dressed like one of the many thousands of homeless men crowding the city, he worked in the downtown east streets. One day, however, he followed a suspect uptown and ran into his aristocratic mother-in-law. "Bill," she said immediately and loudly, "what on earth are you doing dressed like that in public? Go home and change. The suspect heard him and Bill's undercover days were over.

"When World War II broke out, part of him wanted to fight for Canada and join the army immediately. But Babs was pregnant and he couldn't leave her until his daughter was born. He joined the Royal Winnipeg Rifles as a lieutenant in 1941. At first, life in the army seemed like school. He took courses and then came back to his base and taught what he'd learned to his men. Only two years later, in 1943, did Bill and his regiment cross the Atlantic to join the war in Europe. By then, he'd been promoted to captain and had become firm friends with the men he commanded."

After Jo said this, I filled the smart board's screen

with images of 1944 troops training in England as they waited to invade Europe. Jas played the 1940s classic "The White Cliffs of Dover" and after she cut the music, Jo went on, "I've given Dr. Collins the documents and research I've done. I've learned a lot. Most of us know more about what the Americans did on D-Day than we do about our Canadians."

After I projected a map of the Normandy beaches onto the smartboard, Jo used a laser pen when she continued. "Three nations were involved in the invasion of France–Britain, the United States and Canada. The American troops hit these two beaches on the left, Utah and Omaha, and took dreadful casualties — particularly on Omaha. The British landed at Gold, this beach in the middle and at Sword on the right. Sandwiched between was Juno and that's where the Canadians landed. There's one surprising fact about all this, the British had few men killed compared to the Americans and that's partly because they invented all kinds of weird things to help their soldiers transition between the boats and the beach. Not that's that really relevant to my great-grandfather, it's just something interesting."

She cleared her throat and grinned when she continued, "That was fact. This, now, is a Hollywood version of William Carstarphen's Stewart's war."

I killed the screen, Jas stopped the music, and there was absolute quiet as we waited to hear Bill's story.

When Bill rolled up his sleeve for a shot from a medic, he had no idea he'd end up in a British hospital. But once he thought about it, it was typical of life in the army. It didn't go to plan.

Just months earlier, he'd been called into his commanding officer's office. "Bill," Colonel Watts said, "Congratulations. You're the new L.O. for the Canadian forces."

"L.O. sir?"

"Liaison Officer with the British police in all the surrounding villages. You've got police experience. You're popular with the men. When you tell them to get out of a bar and return to base, they jolly well jump to it. With you as L.O. they won't brawl like they've been doing. So, congratulations."

"But, sir," Bill stammered, and then argued till he was blue in the face. He and Babs weren't making the biggest sacrifice of their young marriage for him to become a policeman again. Nothing could change orders from H.Q. though and, unfortunately, the colonel was right. Bill was ideal for the job. A few months later, when he was hospitalized for anaphylactic reaction to the shot, Bill's bed

became the most popular in the hospital. His old unit visited regularly. They laughed and joked around but, after a while, it became clear that the men thought they'd be invading France in a month or two.

"They wouldn't have given us these fancy shots otherwise," one grumbled.

Personally, Bill had thought the army had been trying to keep hospital costs down. But once he pondered it, his men made sense.

As soon as Bill was discharged, he borrowed a car and drove straight to Colonel Watts's office. "My men tell me they're training for invasion."

"Your men are now Captain Naismith's men. They shouldn't be gossiping about operations to you or anyone," Colonel Watts retorted in a cold voice.

Bill blushed. "But are they right, sir? Are we finally going to see war?"

When the colonel didn't say anything, Bill knew the answer. "Colonel, can you get me transferred back here? I don't want to be drinking tea with the Chief Constable when we invade. I signed up to beat Hitler, not to be a glorified cop."

The colonel straightened the pens on his desk. "I understand, Stewart. But you're doing a brilliant job. The Brits have nothing but praise for you."

"I don't want their praise, sir. I want the chance to fight against Hitler with the men I've trained the last three years."

The colonel stood to show that the interview was over. "As I said before, Bill, they're Captain Naismith's men now."

Bill stood his ground. "They say their lieutenant's transferred and that he hasn't been replaced. I volunteer to be that replacement, sir."

The colonel took time making a steeple out of his fingers and holding it to his face. "Bill," he finally said, "I'm not going to demote you. As I said, your work is stellar. And, I certainly can't transfer Naismith. There's not enough time, for one thing."

Bill paced up and down a couple of times while he thought about what he was going to say. "Sir, I can demote myself. Can't I? The question is, will you have me?"

Six months later, on June 6, a Royal Navy transport, crowded with Canadians and their gear, pitched as it climbed one wave after another in the English Channel. Bill leaned against a railing, cursing the weather, as his men hurled whatever their stomachs had left in them into the sea. "It was a dark and stormy night," he muttered to the man beside man.

Back in school, his English teacher had told him that phrase was the worst way to begin a story. Bill now thought the teacher had never met a dark and stormy night. It seemed an ideal beginning.

From what he could gather, so much of their landing on Juno beach in France depended on timing. Battleships were supposed to fire bombardment after bombardment. Tanks would land first and take out the "pill boxes," the concrete towers along the beaches that were manned by Germans planning to gun down invading soldiers.

A naval officer walked by. "Prepare yourself for surprises," he told Bill softly. "We're running at least ten minutes late. The blokes behind us will be even later."

When he left, one of the men stumbled over from the railing. "Sir? You're sure this isn't a training mission? They can't really expect us to invade France in weather like this, can they?"

Bill sympathized with the man. He knew some men were playing high stakes poker below and that bets were being taken whether or not the landing would be called off. Others had found quiet spaces to pray or read their Bibles.

The bombardment stopped. Immediately whistles blew

throughout the ship. "This is it, boys," Bill yelled. "Come on. Get yourselves down to the LCAs."

He knew there'd been a screw-up and that any German officer worth the price of his uniform would know something was about to happen when the ships' guns went silent. "We're nothing but sitting ducks," he muttered to himself.

There was no time to think about anything but hustling his men into their landing craft. As their LCAs ploughed through the rough waves, a gunner beside him threw up all over his battle kit. "Death would be better than this, Captain," he told Bill.

With the bombardment stopped, the quiet was spooky. "That's the navy for you," the gunner complained. "Never where you want them to be. What have they done except deafen us?"

"Feels like waiting for the dentist," someone down from Bill said.

A few more men made jokes to ease the tension as their small craft crept closer to shore. Suddenly gunshots shattered the creepy silence and geysers of water shot up into the air close to the LCA. Bill swallowed. Then a whistle sounded. Bill looked at his watch. Eight o'clock. Fifteen minutes later than planned.

"Get ready," he ordered. "Tighten the straps on your

packs. Make sure your helmet's tight. When they let the ramp down, run like hell. You know what to do. See you on the beach."

His men yelled as they rushed down the ramp into heavy gunfire.

Bill's own shout rivaled theirs for noise as he charged into the cold, cold water.

12

When Jo stopped to take a sip of water, I started flashing images of D-Day landings, mainly from *Storming Juno* and *Saving Private Ryan*. They flashed onto the smartboard one after another, five seconds each, and gave a visual idea of the confusion and terror. Jas simultaneously blasted the noise of gunfire, men's shouts, and the deadly chatter of machine guns through the classroom speakers.

With the pulsating images and the roar of war, something of the horror of 6 June 1944 came through into our genteel classroom. Although it seemed to last forever, it was really only ninety seconds.

But those seconds gave everyone in the room a taste of hell.

When we stopped, the classroom was as spooky quiet as that D-Day morning. As Jo put her bottle of water down, everyone leaned forward in their desks, eager to hear more of her great grandfather's story told Hollywood style.

Bill jumped from the LCA into six or seven feet of water. After he fought his way to the surface, he saw men a few yards away wading through water that was only knee deep and knew he must have landed in a bomb crater. It was the only explanation that made sense. His eighty-pound shoulder pack made swimming difficult and, while he struggled to close the gap between his men and himself, a headless corpse floated by. He almost threw up. He closed his eyes, prayed and continued to push through the water.

A few yards from shore, the Germans had embedded huge barb-like obstacles in the water. They looked gigantic with their long steel arms stretching skyward but Bill was grateful when he sheltered behind one and caught his breath. The noise around him was horrific. Men screamed with pain and one, somewhere, sounded like a dog crying after a car hit it.

Bill cried himself when a soldier from a different company threw himself over a bundle of barbed wire so that his mates could use his back as a bridge. It was so unbe-

lievably heroic and what war was supposed to be all about. Sacrificing yourself for others. Bill knew that, but he'd never expected to see such a vivid illustration of true heroism. Hunkering down in the water, he prepared himself for his dash up the beach when a specially waterproofed tank splashed by. Shouting to his men to follow, Bill chased after the tank as it churned its way through the sand.

The earlier bombing had made the beach itself a mass of craters. Bill swore a couple of times when his feet landed wrongly. But his progress was steady. Around him, bravery seemed an everyday thing as everyone fought to take over the concrete bunkers and machine gun nests along the beach.

It took the Canadians about four hours. By noon the entire Third Division was not only ashore but had captured the resort towns of Courseulles and Bernieres. On the far side of Courseulles, Bill and his men busily stripped the waterproofing off themselves and their tanks. Bill looked up every now and then hoping to see one of his missing men walk in. He'd expected casualties but it hurt to know that at least a third of his men were probably dead already. He had little time to grieve. A dozen men from different units transferred in to bring his Royal Winnipegs up to strength and Colonel Watts told him to "Carry on."

Bill's orders were very specific. He and his men had the

job of taking over the airport at Carpiquet, just outside the major city of Caens. Nothing should stop him from that object. They were not even supposed to fight unless absolutely necessary. High command thought getting Carpiquet airport out of enemy hands as quickly as possible was vital to D-Day's success.

As they settled down to sleep that night, Bill's small group of about forty men had put fifteen miles between themselves and Juno Beach. They had gone deeper into enemy territory than any other Canadian unit and, over breakfast the next morning, June 7, everyone felt confident. German resistance had been much less than anyone had expected. In fact, German troops had been so non-existent that it looked like they'd capture the airport by nightfall. Bill's men sang as they marched along the roads and Bill himself couldn't help but admire the beauty around him. In the fields the wheat, bent down with grain, looked ready for the first cut.

Red poppies lined the roads and dotted the fields. Despite their success so far, Bill couldn't stop his goose bumps when he saw them. John McCrae's 1915 poem flashed into his mind: "In Flanders fields the poppies blow / Between the crosses, row on row."

On either side of him were the fields of Flanders. Pop-

pies moved back and forth in the breeze. He hoped they weren't an omen of bad things to come.

His men didn't have such gloomy thoughts. They had just finished "We'll Meet Again" and seemed bent on singing the entire list of Vera Lynn's songs. Once Bill heard a train in the distance and that reassured him. It was probably heading for Caens and that meant they were going in the right direction.

The relatively easy success at Juno and their fast progress along the French roads made the men feel invincible. "We're here, Gerry," some of them taunted invisible German troops. "Where are you?"

Bill tried to warn them against over-confidence but they wouldn't listen. "We've done the hard part already, sir. We won't see Krauts again till we get to the airport," one man answered, using another wartime nickname for the German army.

Although he told the man to shut up, Bill couldn't stop thinking that he was right. Where was the hand-to-hand fighting he'd been warned to expect? This march resembled a training jaunt along the roads in Scotland more than one in the middle of a war. So when they rounded a bend in the road and gunfire sprayed at them from all directions, the shock paralyzed Bill and his men.

Some dropped to the ground immediately. Outnumbered about five to one, they began to fight but were quickly overwhelmed and rounded up. After a long discussion, the victorious Germans split into two groups. The larger one headed off towards Courseulles; the smaller unit stayed to guard its prisoners of war.

They left a doctor behind and Bill felt grateful when his medics treated the wounded. The fact that he had a wound in his own arm that needed fourteen stitches surprised him. He hadn't even noticed that he was bleeding. He didn't know when it had happened—at Juno, or in the recent fight. He fell to sleep that night a troubled man.

In the morning of 8 June, he felt better. The larks sang, the poppies still bloomed, and their guards treated them well. Just as everyone was finishing breakfast though a few Germans trucks trundled into the yard. Officers got out and about twenty HitlerJugend or Hitler Youth clambered down from the back.

They looked young. Appallingly, so. Though they strutted around the courtyard of the village church pretending that they were seasoned veterans, some might have had their first shave only that morning. When they glared at Bill, their eyes lacked pity.

"They're just kids," Bill said to Ray Morgan, a fellow officer who had transferred in at Courseulles. "They should be in high school."

"Don't underestimate them, Bill. It's bad. I speak a little German, just enough to understand what they're talking about. The guys who captured us are regular army. These thugs," he went on, pointing to the Hitler Youth who stared back at him, "need blooding if they're to fight well. That's what I heard. Their officers are saying that if they shoot us they'll be able to kill in battle. The fact that we're prisoners means nothing to them."

"But we're prisoners of war," Bill stammered. "There's the Geneva Convention."

Ray stared around the courtyard of the church that was their temporary prison. "And Kurt Meyer, their Major General, has told them not to take prisoners. That means we have to non-exist."

"I don't believe it," Bill said. But as he looked at the teenagers guarding his men, he began to feel Ray might be right. Shortly afterwards the regular troops who had captured them the day before marched out. Immediately, the HitlerJugend officers barked orders and their boys began pushing Bill's men towards a road.

"March," one ordered.

Some picked up the stretchers the wounded were on and slowly the group began to walk. There were no poppies to brighten the way now and Bill's stomach roiled. He thought of the last letter his little Barbie had sent.

"Hurry home, Daddy," she'd written. "It's almost summer and Mommy says you'll teach me to swim." Then she had added, "I can't really remember what you look like but I love you and you're my very own hero."

Bill didn't feel like much of a hero. He hadn't kept his men out of harm's way. After they were forced over railroad tracks and into yet another field, he knew it was the end. The German officers shouted orders and Ray told the men to kneel in a square, the wounded in the middle.

Hoping that his body would shield some of the men behind, Bill knelt in the front row as tall as he could. "They'll shoot us first," he shouted back to his friends. "You, at the back. As soon as you hear the guns, run like hell and hide in the wheat. If you're lucky, you'll get a chance."

He thought of little Barbie and his beautiful wife, Babs and the words he used when he'd proposed to her. "You're still my east and west, my moonlight on a tranquil sea," he murmured to himself.

Somewhere behind him, a man started singing the twenty-third Psalm. More and more men joined in, and when they reached the second verse, Bill did as well: "Yea, though I walk in death's dark…."

Jo stopped.

I flashed a picture of crosses in the Beny-sur-Mer cemetery and Jas sent the sharp rapid sounds of machine guns throughout the classroom.

"Kurt Meyer's Hitler Jugend murdered my great-grandfather on 8 June 1944," Jo finished with tears in her voice. "His war lasted fifty-some hours. I wish I'd known him."

Somewhere behind me someone sobbed and no one felt like talking.

When I got to school the next morning, Jas grabbed me immediately. "Are you coming to the house for the weekend?"

Honestly, I hadn't thought about it. "I don't know. Wherever I am, I have to do school work. It's piling up with playoffs and another trip back east."

Jas looked troubled. "I know. I'm in the same boat." She started pleating her sleeve—a sure sign that she was worried about something. "But, Jenn, I need a huge favor."

A huge favor? Jas? The I'm-so-independent Jas?

"Ask away." The warning bell sounded, so I added, "And, whatever it is, hurry up."

"You know how I'm sort of Jewish," she blurted out. "I don't know anything about being Jewish. I sort of wondered if you'd go to Jewish church with me on Saturday."

The fact that Jewish church was on Saturday morning basically covered my knowledge of Jewishness. I didn't even know if outsiders were welcome. "Can we?" I asked. "Don't you have to be Jewish to go?"

Jas started moving and we headed for math class. "I don't know. But if we can, will you go with me?"

I tried to picture it but couldn't. I had absolutely no idea what Jewish church meant. I knew several Jewish girls in school but they weren't really my friends.

The idea of Jewish church petrified me. I knew some Christian churches asked people to get up and introduce themselves. If the Jewish church was like that, would I have the guts to say, "Hi, I'm Jennifer North and my great-great-grandfather stopped your relatives from coming to Canada?"

Jas got out her phone and I guess she Googled Jewish church policy because she looked frustrated. "It's complicated," she whispered.

Inside myself, I sighed with relief. "Wait for Toronto," I told her. "Ask the Halders to take you when we go for the tournament."

When we flew to Toronto, it was a blur. Party, party, party, to celebrate the sister-school thing. I didn't mind them but they were tiring. As I expected, Prim Heights was now partnered with Mandy's school. What none of us expected was that the directors of the volleyball tournament had only invited schools who had won championships. Besides our hosts, there was another Toronto school, three more Ontario schools and two from the United States. After our first game, we knew we were in tough.

Jas didn't score our games. She didn't have to. There were officially qualified scorers. She sat in the stands between her mother and mine with the Halders huddled behind them and everything seemed fine.

I was about to serve for the game when I noticed the Dicksons walking towards the group. Wondering what would happen, I kept bouncing the ball until I got a delay of game warning.

"Jenn," Jo whispered and glared and me. "Concentrate. Just get the ball in, won't you?"

My serve went in and we won that game but had to play another for the set. I couldn't stop myself from sneaking glances over at Jas and Mom. Nobody looked angry. They cheered when we won a point but I couldn't stop thinking about them.

I didn't have time to find out anything after the match, either. News of Jo's tennis prowess must have leaked out somehow—think Grandmother—and she and I were asked to play a "friendly" game at a local club.

We looked at each other. Didn't anyone realize that we'd just played three sets of volleyball? Jo quirked her eyebrow at me and I nodded.

We borrowed racquets and looked ridiculous playing in our volleyball uniforms and shoes in a club where everyone else wore white. A surprising number of people watched us from an upstairs bar. I'd expected Mom and Jo's dad but Cousin Mandy was a surprise as were about twenty other girls and ten or so teacher-looking people.

Coach Copeland would have been proud of my backhand. Once it became obvious that it was our weak point, our opponents attacked and attacked it. A lot of times I resorted to topspin lobs just to give myself time to recover.

Afterwards Jo and I went for dinner by ourselves with our parents. Mom couldn't believe my tennis. "Jenn," she said, "where have you been? A tennis player? I never thought you could possibly be so good."

I rolled my eyes. "Didn't you listen when I moaned and groaned about Coach Copeland? She's been pounding me for a couple of months."

Mr. Carruthers looked at Jo. "Ms. Copeland's seriously good, Jo. I don't think I could afford to pay for that kind of coaching. You're being given a huge gift."

Mom chimed in along those lines and I thought as I ate. Because neither Jo nor I cared about tennis, we'd been given top calibre coaching for free. Even if I quit tomorrow, I'd received a lifelong gift from Coach Copeland. I'd seen all kinds of eighty year old tennis players but none who still played volleyball or basketball. That's what it was. A lifelong gift.

"Stop frowning, Jenn," Mom said suddenly. "You've had a good day. You've got into the next round at the tournament and you and Jo just beat the Ontario junior champs."

I shrugged. Beating another champion tennis pair hadn't been on my list when I got up. Mr. Carruthers laughed at my face. "You know, the most extraordinary thing is that you two have no idea how good you are. That was what everyone said today. You're two very special tennis players. No one believed me when I told them the only reason you're playing at all is because you decided a friend had to go to a dance."

Mom nodded. "Your friendship and your tennis are the only good things to come out of our family mess, Jenn. I was right when I insisted that you stayed at Prim Heights."

And that led into the reason for the match. Grandmother had managed to rave about Jo's tennis in all the right places and our new sister school had decided to poach Jo. As Grandmother told them that Jo would only play with me, the so-called "friendly" was really my audition. Grandmother wanted me in Toronto with Mom and Dad. Jo had just been collateral damage.

I felt angry for Mom because I felt that Grandmother was pressuring her to stay with Dad. I couldn't tell what was happening there. I didn't see much of Dad but what did I expect? Our quality time would consist of one lunch together. One lunch? I saw more of Jo's dad than my own that weekend.

The tournament finished late Saturday night when we lost to St. Bridget's, a Detroit school. Although we fought hard, we had nothing left. I think that the result would have been the same though if St. Bridget's had done the traveling and played at Prim Heights. There was no doubt about it. They were better than us.

Sunday morning was a whirlwind. Grandmother hosted a huge brunch. Mandy and her parents came, Jo and her dad, Jas and her mom, plus the Dicksons and the Halders. I sort of expected to see Cecil but Jas had found out that neither he nor his parents had stepped foot in Grandmother's house since the Thanksgiving incident.

Halfway through her brunch, Grandmother asked Mom where she was going to spend Christmas. It was obvious from Mom's face that she hadn't decided but Grandmother had forced the issue.

"Qualicum Beach," Mom retorted with a warlike glint in her eye.

"Right here," Dad said at the same moment as though there could be no other answer.

Everyone went quiet. Jas and Jo shifted so that they sort of buttressed me. Grandmother, though, was equal to the occasion. "How many bedrooms do you have?" she asked Mom.

"It depends on Dave and Don. I haven't discussed Christmas with them but if they came out we'd have two spare guest rooms in the house. There's a guest cottage, as well."

Grandmother didn't blink an eye. "Is the cottage heated?"

I wished I could see Mom's face but Dad had hunched forward. Mom took her time before answering, "Yes. But you might be more comfortable in the main house. There's an excellent suite upstairs."

Grandmother nodded her head in agreement and

there was a subdued gasp before Mandy blurted out, "May I come too? Please?"

QBeach was suddenly the place to be. The only person who didn't seem enthusiastic about a Christmas there was Dad. In a way, I felt sorry for him. He must have felt that Grandmother had deserted his ship.

He drove us to the airport, and for that I was grateful. I had no idea if he and Mom were even together but I still wanted to be his little girl. It seemed so long since he'd done something fun with me. The quality time lunch wasn't worth anything.

I was still moping about Dad when Jas nestled in beside me on the plane. Jo sat next to her and, just like that, we were back to being our own little family of three again.

I didn't say anything and I assumed they were watching something on the vid screen but Jas tapped my arm, "Your grandmother's roasted about coming out at Christmas. She asked Mom all kinds of questions about what to bring. I think this is her way of telling your dad that he's a jerk."

That was a thought. "I only wish you could come to QBeach with the rest of us."

Jas's smile was warm and sunny. "We're having our own family Christmas. Hanukkah too, because all the Halders are coming out. Grandmother said she's going to have a big party to introduce Mom and me to her friends and that I could invite all of mine to come as well."

She stopped for a moment and frowned. "When I said my friends were only you and Jo, and maybe Axel and Mike, Grandfather sat me down and told me he thought I'd become very popular as soon as people found out that I'm his granddaughter. He insisted that I had to learn to deal with that instant popularity."

Jo shifted in her seat so that she could join the conversation. "He's right, Jas. You'll be invited to all kinds of things. I don't want to hurt you but you'll have to remember that the invitations will really be for your grandparents' money. I hope he told you to be careful."

Jo pleated the little airline blanket we'd been given. "Don't forget I'm still officially a scholarship kid. Till tomorrow, anyway. I know who the snobs at Prim Heights are and I remember every nasty thing they've ever said to me."

I felt very uncomfortable. Until Mom forced it on me, I hadn't been friends with Jas. She seemed to know what I was thinking because she grinned at me. "Don't worry, Jenn. You're good. Never think that I don't appreciate the hours you spend slaving away at tennis. I know it all has something to do with getting me to the dance. You have no idea what that means to me."

Fortunately the flight attendants came by with the drinks trolley and by the time they'd gone the embarrassing moment was over.

Jo nudged Jas. "Listen, before you go asleep on us, talk about your project. We've only got till Thursday to pull it together."

"Last class, fortunately," Jas said with a grin. "Everyone will be tired but the story's incredible. When Grandfather was a little boy, he left Austria on the very day that Hitler invaded. He said his mother never expected to see his father again and the story of my great grandfather's escape is too wild to be made up. It's pure fantasy."

I reached across and pulled her earplugs out of the seat. "No more movies or music until you tell us. If it's as good as you say it's better than the movie choices."

13

It was easier this time. I knew how to set up the computers and Jo took her chair beside me. I started with pictures of Austrian Alps, the city of Vienna, and intermingled them with images of art by Gustav Klimt, Chaim Soutine, Picasso and Cezzane. Jo played the Viennese Waltz by Johannes Strauss II and the class looked puzzleded. Dr. Collins doodled with a pen.

Then Jas entered, looking mysterious and somehow glamorous in black. As soon as she reached the front we killed the pictures and music. In the quiet, she began. "At the St. Nick's tennis dance, something very strange happened. I sat next to my grandfather."

Someone made a choked noise as though she wondered how a scholarship girl's grandfather could afford the dance. Then Jas dropped her bombshell.

"When I said strange it was because I didn't know who he was, much less that he was my grandfather. Nor did I know that I'm partly Jewish."

Everyone gasped but seemed divided. For some the fact that Jas had not known her grandparents was the shock. For others, of course, I guess it was because of her Jewishness. Jas had always been so out there with her Anglicanism. When they settled again, she said, "This is the story of my great-grandfather, Raphael Wolff-Jaegar's escape from the Nazis in March, 1938. Like Jo, I'm going to tell it as a story. It will be a trifle long but I have incredible proof to show you at the end. My great-grandfather's story starts on New Year's Eve, 1934 in a skiing resort called Garnish-Partenkirchen in Bavaria."

Raphael Wolff-Jaegar squinted as he studied himself in the mirror. His black tie was not right. Ordinarily his valet would have tied it for him but Raffa had left him behind in Vienna after his friends talked him into skiing the newly opened Olympic runs in Germany.

He felt uncomfortable in Nazi-controlled territory. He'd hemmed and hawed about it but the chance to test out the new runs had been the difference because Raffa knew he wouldn't be allowed to attend the Winter Games in 1936. Not with the way things were going politically.

He squinted again and shrugged his shoulders. He'd already retied the thing six times and this was his best attempt. Would anyone notice in the dim light of the hotel's ballroom? Of course, someone would. A Wolff-Jaegar was a Wolff-Jaegar and no matter where they went in the world, they were always on show.

Swearing softly, he pulled the tie apart and had just started on his seventh attempt when someone pounded on his door. Thinking it might be one of his friends and hoping that friend might be a bow tie expert, Raffa smiled as he opened the door.

The smile faded when he found himself face to face with the hotel manager.

"Herr Wolff-Jaegar. Please. You're needed," the man blurted out, almost falling into the room in his anxiety. "Sir, we have four missing skiers and a blizzard is predicted. Already we have a few volunteers out but we need experts for the high runs. Sir, will you head up a team?"

He'd miss the New Year's Gala, Raffa thought immediately. But there was no other choice. "I'll get my own team. Wexler, Baumann and Landau," he assured the manager knowing he could count on his friends.

Three grueling hours later, Raffa looked down at the

town's twinkling lights from atop one of the new runs. They looked so cheery and no one seeing them would guess there was a world-wide depression. Only a few years earlier men had jumped from offices high above Wall Street, New York and desperate Berliners had traded cart-loads of paper money for loaves of bread. Still, people always wanted a chance to party and New Year's Eve was the perfect opportunity to wish for something better. One night's joy in exchange for 364 days of pain.

His team also had good reason to celebrate. It had covered almost every inch of its assigned area and found three of the missing skiers. After Joe Landau and Adam Baumann started shepherding them down to the first aid station, Leo Wexler came back for Raffa.

"Come on," he implored. "If we go now, we can still make the party. The end of it, anyway."

"You go. There's no sense in both of us missing it. I'll follow as soon as I've checked Mueller's Corner," Raffa answered as his eyes combed the mountain again. Cloud-shrouded trees cast eerie shadows, ones so dark that even a sweep of light from their lanterns couldn't penetrate their thickness.

Mueller's Corner was a notorious gully. To the eye of an inexperienced skier, it looked like a pleasant, treed shortcut between beginners' runs. Although warning signs *were everywhere, the Corner managed to snare victim after victim because skiers, if they weren't already turning when they came to it, would crash onto the bare rocks fifteen feet below.*

Raffa respected the Corner and approached it cautiously. He cursed the moon as it slid behind clouds and wondered why he was being so conscientious. An earlier rescue crew had examined it from the precipice and found nothing. Why did he feel it necessary to personally search it?

Sidestepping his way carefully around the boulders guarding its entrance, Raffa found exactly what he had expected. Snow-covered rocks, snow-covered rocks, and more rocks. Poking the large ones with his pole, he reached the far end of the canyon and looked back. Even with the help of his lantern, it was hard to distinguish rocks from shadows. He scanned the area carefully again and his eyes almost jumped from their sockets when he saw a broken ski jutting above one of the rocks almost right in front of him.

A snow-covered mound lay atop one of the boulders. Taking his own skis off and supporting himself with his poles, Raffa climbed until he was slightly above it. He'd found the last skier. One of his legs looked broken but not disastrously. Raffa gently brushed a layer of snow from his face and checked his pulse. It was faint and erratic and

Raffa knew that just keeping the man alive would take all his skill.

He blew his emergency whistle three times—the pre-arranged signal that the lost skier had been found. After counting to fifteen, he blew again and, when he heard nothing but the wind flirting with the snow on the top of the gully he shouted for help, hoping against hope that Wexler was still in earshot. Only then reluctantly, and very reluctantly, did he accept the fact that he was on his own.

He lifted the skier into a sitting position. The man gave an anguished yelp and Raffa knew he'd jarred the broken leg. Pain, however, didn't snap the man out of his unconsciousness and knowing that he was in a race against hypothermia Raffa quickly put his own jacket and sweater over the man. Taking his gloves off, he massaged the skier's icy-cold chest while blowing warm breath into the man's mouth.

It seemed an eternity but it was probably only a few minutes before he felt a change. As the skier's pulse steadied somewhat, Raffa looked for the broken skis. If he could rebreak them into the right size they'd make excellent splints and while he mashed them against a rock Raffa decided to name the man Bruno. Bruno would give him someone to talk to.

"It's a good job these are wood, Bruno," he said, hacking

Bruno's jacket into two and ripping its sleeves off. "Anything sturdier and I might not be able to help your leg."

He picked up one of the improvised splints and checked Bruno's pulse. Though terribly weak, it was steady. Taking a deep breath, Raffa pulled the broken leg back into alignment as best he could. Ignoring Bruno's agonized shouts, he quickly splinted it and used the hacked-off jacket sleeves as ties. Then he wrapped the rest of Bruno's jacket around the leg for cushioning and tied his scarf tightly around everything.

Although Bruno had protested a couple more times during the process, he hadn't snapped out of oblivion. Raffa was glad for that. The trip down the mountain would be a nightmare if Bruno regained consciousness. Satisfied that he'd done as much as he could, Raffa hoisted Bruno over his shoulder in a fireman's lift and set off.

The next hour tested his endurance to its limit. Though he was thin, Bruno became unbearably heavy and to distract himself Raffa began talking, using the time to work through his thoughts about his family's current crisis.

"Obviously," he told the unconscious Bruno, "nobody's going to challenge Hitler. Not yet, anyway. Every day something new is prohibited or restricted. He's abolished the unions and made it impossible for Jewish doctors and lawyers to earn good livings. The brightest Jews have *already left Germany for America. Even Professor Einstein."*

He paused to catch his breath and blew his whistle three more times. When there was no answer, he adjusted Bruno and resumed walking. "No matter what anyone says I believe Austria will be one of his targets. Stands to reason. Dozens, if not hundreds, of Austrians join the Nazis every day. At least half of the country would welcome a Hitler takeover. And that's my problem, Bruno. We haven't met but if we did, you'd know I'm Austrian and a Jew. I'm proud of both and wouldn't change either. But it doesn't mean that I don't see what's happening."

As he stumbled over a mogul, Raffa almost lost his grip on Bruno and once again he was glad the man remained unconscious. Any jolt would have been pure agony. To make matters worse the weather changed with snow falling and blotting out signposts. Raffa fished goggles out of a back pocket and his pace was slower as he struggled forward.

"Most of my family is blind to any danger," he went on. "They say we're too rich, too well known for anything to happen to us. Look at the Rothschilds, they tell me. They've survived through thick and thin."

He felt strangely peaceful as he talked his problem out. He'd adjusted to Bruno's weight and worked himself into a rhythm. The air felt crisp, not icy cold, and his thoughts about the family meeting now less than forty hours away were crystalizing. Even the snow was beautiful as it covered the trees lining the run.

"Comparing us to the Rothschilds is stupid and dangerous. Their product is money and money can drift around the world, sticking here, making a profit there. It doesn't matter whether the home office is Berlin, Vienna or New York. The Rothschilds will prosper wherever.

"But our wealth comes from manufacturing and we're exceptionally rich. Not Rothschild-level rich, but just below it. We make cotton. The finest you can buy and we can't magically transport acres of mills to vacant land in America or Australia. Neither can we suddenly convert them into diamonds and sneak them out of Austria. It can't be done. So we'll have to be terribly creative to keep any money out of Hitler's clutches."

He was nearly at the bottom of the run and he fought exhaustion and the temptation to speed up. He resumed his one-sided conversation and found it steadied his pace. "I've got a plan but it will only get some of our money out and we'll need years to make it happen. The problem is that I don't know if we have enough of those years."

Exhaustion forced him into another stop and

when Raffa blew his whistle again, he heard a long blast back. He yelled and heard answering voices.

"Not long now, Bruno, my friend," he said, setting off with a much brisker step. "There are people waiting to look after you. They'll get you all the help you need."

The following morning Raffa felt like he'd been in a train wreck. If he'd had another day's grace before the family meeting, he'd have stayed in bed. Instead he had a long drive back to Vienna in front of him.

He took time while settling his bill at the front desk to enquire after Bruno. Apparently, he was resting comfortably in hospital and the manager's smile was proud, almost as though he'd rescued Bruno himself, when he praised Raffa's splinting of the broken leg. "The doctors said they probably could not have done a better job themselves in the circumstances."

As he put his wallet back into his jacket pocket, Raffa felt absurdly gratified. He thought of the Christians' Golden Rule: "Do unto others, as you would have them do for you." Well, he'd done unto another what he hoped someone would do for him in a similar circumstance.

Walking towards the door he stopped and his smile disappeared when he heard a woman's shrill voice. "I don't care if he's the best ski instructor in Germany. He's a Jew. As soon as I found out, I pulled our Hilda out of his clutches immediately. What's more, I told the manager to get every single stinking Jew out of the resort. I don't want it contaminated." She glanced around the hotel lobby and then took a couple of steps towards Raffa and held out her hand. "You agree with me, sir?"

Raffa looked into her eyes and saw ignorance and hatred. Then he smiled with all the charm he possessed. "Certainly, madam. In fact, I'm leaving right now so that I won't be contaminated."

Jas stopped talking and smiled. "I bet you're wondering what this has to do with World War II, aren't you? Well, I warned you that my story was longer than Jo's. If you want to stretch, this is the time. When I start again, you'll get the connection." I didn't bother getting up. I simply rotated my shoulders to ease the tension.

Back in Vienna, Raffa strode into the Wolff-Jaeger board room. Ignoring his aching back and quadriceps, he took his place at the head of the table. Other family members sat on either side, their expressions ranging from bore-

dom through glum to anxious. Only Uncle Jacob seemed friendly.

As Raffa outlined the crisis the family faced, a couple of the faces became stony. "We've got nothing to fear. We can survive," Uncle Abram insisted. "The king of England wears our cotton. We'll just stick it out. Nobody will touch us."

Great-Uncle Zamuel looked worried but he nodded assent. "I agree, but it wouldn't hurt to make a really big donation to the Nazi Party. Something people will remember and talk about. And maybe, we should have young ..." He broke off and frowned as he struggled to remember. "You know, young whats-his-name, the one that married little Leah. Maybe he should join the Party and make himself important. Goodness knows, he does nothing else."

Across the table Uncle Jacob's eyes flashed fire. "A Wolff-Jaegar join a political party that thinks Jews are vermin. You cannot be serious, Zamuel."

"Money talks, Jacob," Great-Uncle Zamuel replied and his face looked as obstinate as a mule's. "If we make our gift big enough, even Hitler won't forget us."

"You can count on that," Uncle Jacob countered. "We're Jews. His chosen enemy. He'll laugh all the way to the bank and then he'll take our mills. You don't believe me?

Then, one of you buy my share in the company. If you're so confident in the future, buy me out. I'll even give a family discount."

Raffa looked around the table as each man considered the offer. Some of them looked down at their leather-bound red placemats and fiddled with their pens. Others stared at the paneled walls as though hoping one of them would swing open and provide a magical place of safety. He was about to respond when Uncle Jacob stood and sneered at his relatives.

"No takers. I thought not. Well, I'm through. I've got a few years left and somehow the Bahamas seem a safe place to spend them. As for my company shares? They're yours, Raphael. Free and clear." He pushed his chair back and started for the door.

"Sit down, Uncle Jacob," Raffa said, asserting his authority. "We're not finished and you're not finished with the company. I've got a plan. A workable one, I think. But it's going to take time and all of us working together to pull it off."

While Uncle Jacob resumed his seat, the others looked at Raffa when he continued, "I think it's inevitable that Austria will become Nazi. So many people here approve of Hitler. He's decisive. He does things. He's giving back the pride that took such a beating in the Great War.

He makes us forget those harsh years." As Great-Uncle Zamuel nodded, Raffa put up three fingers. "Pride. Hope. Progress. Three unbeatable things."

"And things our politicians just bleat about," Uncle Abram said. "That's why I think we should throw in our lot with him."

"We can't, Uncle. We're Jews, although the last time you went to synagogue was for Isaak's bar-mitzvah." There were a few snickers. Uncle Abram was more likely to be found in the Kirche St. Gertrud than the synagogue.

"I think we must safeguard ourselves," Raffa went on, "by putting as much of our money in foreign banks as we can."

"And how are you going to do that? My banker tells me there's already a watch on our accounts," Uncle Jacob said. "That's one reason I want to take everything that I can right now and go far away. It's only going to get worse."

"I agree," Raffa nodded. "So here's the plan. We do the expected thing and get as many assets into Switzerland as we can. That's the easiest and the most convenient. If trouble comes, the Swiss will stay out of it. That's the only thing we can bank on. But we have to do more. Far more. I fear this popularity of Hitler's and his tendency to use brute force to persuade people when his words fail. I think we have to get the bulk of our money away from Europe."

"Where?" Uncle Zamuel asked, his face showing interest for the first time since Raffa had begun.

"America."

There was silence while the nine men thought about America. Most of them had visited New York and thought it unsophisticated when compared to Vienna, Paris or London.

"I know what you're thinking," Raffa said. "But New York has one huge advantage. The Atlantic Ocean. Hitler might be able to invade England but I doubt that he has a navy big enough to take on the Americans."

Again there was silence. "The Americans think the Great War cost them too much. They won't rush to fight another one," Uncle Abram said shrewdly. "They'll stay out of it. I see your point though, Raphael. Yes, indeed. New York might be safer than Zurich."

"So the question is how. How do we manage it?" Great-Uncle Zamuel asked.

"How do we send money out of the country now?" Raffa asked.

"Bill payments," Uncle Abram said.

"And where does most of that money go?"

"Egypt. It grows the cotton. We buy, spin and weave it."

"Exactly. Now, uncles, listen carefully. There's risk involved in my plan," Raffa said. "I need you to think this through and see if there's something I haven't thought of. Bear in mind, this is a five year plan. Seven years would be better but I can't see us having that much time."

Great-Uncle Zamuel's interest got the better of him. "Go on, man," he implored. "Get to it."

"Well, my plan has two parts. Let's deal with the Egyptian one first. I think we should bribe someone there to double-bill us for everything. One account should be sent to us here in Vienna; the other should go to our office in Alexandria."

"We don't have an office there," Great-Uncle Zamuel objected immediately.

"Yet," Raffa answered and smiled. "Remember young what's-his-name, young Leah's husband, the do-nothing? Let's send him to Alexandria and set him up as a prince. I'll personally guarantee to get Leah and his children out of here if trouble comes. We'll give him the responsibility of sending the money we pay for that dummy bill to a bank in New York. The books should look all right. We'll have one bill sent to us here and we pay that back to Egypt. The second one goes to the Alexandria and it's supposedly paid out of our bank account there. Every quarter, we send

down money to keep the office going and to cover the bills that go to it."

The uncles started figuring our numbers on their blotters. "If we can do that for five years," Uncle Jacob said, "we'll have a considerable amount of money."

"It gets better with part two," Raffa said with a smile. "I'm so glad you volunteered to oversee the new office in America, Uncle Jacob."

"I said Nassau, not New York," he answered immediately.

"So you fly in once a month? Stay at the Waldorf? What a sacrifice," Raffa countered. "Now here's the rest of the plan. I want to get new suppliers, American ones. I know their prices are sky high compared to our Egyptian supplier but we can double-bill there as well. It will be much harder to keep track of our New York money, I assure you. What do you say, uncles? Are you in?"

"In," Uncle Jacob said.

"In," Great-Uncle Zamuel agreed. "It's cheaper than giving a donation to the Nazis. So, yes, I'm in. Just tell me what you want."

What a difference hope made, Raffa thought as he looked around the room. His uncles' faces were bright and he could see their brains whirring away as they thought of squirreling the Wolff-Jaegar assets away from harm.

"So here's the cost," he said. "Uncle Jacob? You and I will leave for New York as soon as possible and open a trust account as well as a company one. Uncle Abram, would you be willing to relocate to Zurich and handle everything there? I want someone's visible presence in the city just in case the banks get too creative with our money."

Both uncles nodded.

"And me?" Great-Uncle Zamuel said. "It sounds like I should be the caretaker right here in Vienna. If worst comes to worst like you think and we have to get out, I'll be the one to stay behind. What's the worst they can do to me, an old man? Put me in prison?"

14

Jas stopped for a glass of water. "It's now the twelfth of March, 1938 and this is the rest of the story."

Raffa watched the taillights of the family's Mercedes sedan until they disappeared around the bend leading to the Czech border. He lit a cigarette. He waited, and waited. After an hour, he turned his Mercedes coupe around and headed back to Vienna feeling like his heart was now in a foreign country.

The Nazis had invaded his beloved Vienna. He had kept his promise and sent Leah and her family out the day before and now he'd sent Ruthie, his wife, and his son Thell to safety as well. He'd only gone to the border to make sure the driver didn't lose his nerve and turn back.

Apparently, the small fortune he'd paid had done the trick. It might have been the best investment he'd ever made.

It was quiet going back into Vienna. All the traffic was going the other way—cars and carts of every description—and Raffa could only pray that he'd be in that long line the following afternoon. He only needed a few more hours to get the rest of the business details finished. His uncles had overruled his suspicions about their new lawyer and Raffa couldn't blame them. He couldn't say or put his finger on exactly what was wrong with the man.

It was a matter of trust and Raffa didn't trust him.

And then he had to make decisions about the art. That was the problem with owning treasures. A lot of Austrians believed the Wolff-Jaegar art collection belonged to them. The famous Gustav Klimt portrait of his mother was just one example. Although his father had commissioned and paid for it, people persisted in thinking that it belonged to them in a museum. They might have different opinions as to which museum but they were united in thinking it didn't belong in the Wolff-Jaegar house. Raffa understood some of their feelings because the portrait was a masterpiece.

But they had to realize it was his mother, damn it.

Worse, besides being so well known, the portrait was huge. Too big for him to take out of the country. That's what he'd told his favourite art dealer earlier. "I can't take it with me. Can you get it copied? Then, if the Nazis want it give them the fake and hide the real one. We'll be back as soon as the trouble's over. In the meantime," he'd gone on, handing across a small Cezanne, "keep this for your trouble."

That was one more chore for the following morning. He'd go back to see if the dealer had been successful. What he really needed was the best art counterfeiter in Vienna but Raffa didn't have a clue about finding him. He fretted about the dealer's honesty as well. Did he value the Cezanne and future Wolff-Jaegar business enough to keep the Klimt and other treasures out of Nazi hands?

The last thing he had to do was persuade his favorite cousin to leave with him. He and Adele were the same age. They'd grown up together, holidayed together, but lately Adele had changed. She refused to believe that the Nazis were evil, saying the rumours about them were nothing but Jewish hysteria. It would be a wasted effort but, at least, he would have tried. He soothed himself by the fireplace with a glass of whisky. He smoked a cigar and tried to relax but he couldn't stop himself from remembering the famous remark by a British earl on the eve of the Great War. "The lights are going out all over Europe," Earl Grey had said in 1914. Raffa didn't know about Europe but as he read-

ied himself for bed he knew his own world would never be the same.

He had just begun to doze off when the dull thunder of soldiers marching made his adrenaline race. "Keep going by," he prayed. "Almighty God, give me one more day or just one more morning, even one good hour."

The men's feet stamped out to an emphatic stop. The sound of the knocker against his front door reverberated throughout the house. He stuck his head outside the bedroom window and his heart dropped when he saw a detail of thirty Nazis. "One moment," he called down and then dressed in his best business clothes. While he might be arrested and possibly interned, he was still Raphael Wolff-Jaegar.

Twenty-four hours later, Raffa lay awake in his cell. He supposed that he should be grateful. At least he was by himself. Some cells around him were crowded—or so he deduced. He knew most of his fellow prisoners. They were Vienna's elite: its top doctors, professors, lawyers, businessmen. No, that wasn't quite true. They were Vienna's top Jewish doctors, professors, lawyers and businessmen.

But even that wasn't true. Although his Jewish friends were in the majority, there were others. But for every well-dressed acquaintance, Raffa had seen communists and other malcontents with battered, bloody faces. Obviously, their arrests hadn't been as "civilized" as his own.

Raffa thought about Ruthie and Thell. Part of him exulted because they had escaped; another part fretted and couldn't believe they were safe. If everything had gone according to plan, they would have travelled on to Switzerland and now be ensconced in a Zurich hotel. By now, though, Ruthie would be guessing that something bad had happened to him.

"Get a tourist visa. Fly first class to London. Stay at the Dorchester, Ruthie, and wear your jewelry. Don't look like a refugee. I'll find you there. I promise," he murmured to himself, going over the sentences he'd made Ruthie memorize. Then he began whispering over and over, "Keep to the plan, Ruthie, keep to the plan. I don't know how, but I'll find you. I promise."

He was still whispering when the lights dimmed and, judging by the tossing and turning sounds, the men around him prepared themselves for sleep. He took his jacket off and lay on the bed thinking sleep would be far away. However, it seemed he had only just closed his eyes when he woke to the sounds of men outside his cell and the noise of his door being unlocked.

Four Nazis entered. Their oberscharfuher, or sergeant, bellowed, "Get up. Right now. Immediately."

The squad shuffled and stamped their feet impatiently as Raffa slowly combed his hair, wishing he had fresh water to wash away the grime that he felt on his face. As soon as he'd put his suit jacket on, the sergeant grabbed his arms, shackled his feet and put handcuffs around his wrists.

"This way. Smartly now," the sergeant ordered and roughly pushed Raffa out of his cell.

"Keep your wits sharp," one of Raffa's friends shouted. "Watch every word you say. They come for the worst cases at midnight. Be prepared."

"God be with you," another shouted before breaking into loud prayers.

As they walked the hallways, Raffa studied his captors. Austrian Nazis, he decided, judging from their shirts and black jodhpur-type pants stuffed into long black boots. They marched as though they were drilling. Each step had an authoritative stamp to it and they wheeled around corners with precision.

They were "brownshirts"—men who had joined the Nazi Party and done whatever the Party wanted. A riot? Certain citizens beaten up? No problem. For many of them, being a Nazi made them feel significant and that was what Raffa sensed as they pushed him along the hallways to a staircase. Taking him to wherever he was going was probably the most important job they'd ever had.

When they left the cell blocks, the paint changed. It seemed a silly detail to notice but it stuck in his mind. His cell and the hallways surrounding it had been whitewashed. Now, as he climbed higher, more expensive paint covered the walls. Though still utilitarian—grey and dull greens—it was the same quality he used in his own cellars.

At ground level, they stopped while the sergeant consulted the guard detail at the door. After he'd shuffled through the door, Raffa couldn't believe how luxurious the fresh air felt. Although he'd been imprisoned for a little more than twenty-four hours, his sense of smell had adjusted to the lingering stink of vomit and urine in the prison block. He breathed deeply and then noticed a transport truck surrounded by heavily armed men at the curb.

His escort and the transport team saluted each other and shouted "Heil Hitler" several times before the back canvas opened and Raffa was hauled into the truck. It then set off on such an erratic course that he had no sense of where he was. Occasionally he heard angry shouts, the staccato of gunfire, and the sounds of people running but he had no idea if they were coming from a riot or from people resisting arrest. Further on he heard loud cheering that seemed to go on forever. There had been rumours that Adolph Hitler himself would come to Vienna. Had this happened already? Was this cheering the German Fuhrer's welcome?

Eventually the truck stopped and Raffa pondered his chances of escaping. All he would need was a distraction—like the sounds he had just heard.

But as he laboriously climbed down everything was peaceful. The brownshirts took a moment to brush themselves off almost as though they were going on parade. To Raffa's astonishment, one of them roughly pulled bits of straw from Raffa's rumpled suit.

Why was it so important that he look his best?

He was still trying to work this out when they began marching again. He was in the middle with the sergeant out in front, a brownshirt on either side of him and one behind his back. Although escape seemed impossible, his spirits lightened when he recognized his surroundings. He was being escorted through a side entrance to the City Hall.

As he marched along marble floors to the main staircase, Raffa again looked for an escape route and bitterly noticed that red, black and white Nazi flags were everywhere. Nazi colored streamers garlanded every pillar. He wouldn't count on getting help from anyone in this building.

When the marble floors gave way to thick, luxurious carpet, Raffa wasn't much surprised when they stopped in front of the mayor's office. The sergeant deferentially knocked on the door, spoke briefly to an aide and then removed Raffa's shackles and handcuffs.

"We wait," he grunted, as though he owed some kind of explanation

The waiting lasted forever. Raffa knew it was a tactic designed to exhaust prisoners and make them lose hope. He endured the time by thinking of Ruthie and Thell in their Zurich hotel room and by preparing himself as best he could for the coming interrogation.

The Nazis would want control of the family's mills and every other Wolff-Jaegar enterprise. They'd want to know where his family was, how to access all the Wolff-Jaegar bank accounts, how to get their hands on the company's shares, and who was in charge of each business. They'd had a day to work on their strategy and Raffa wondered exactly how much they knew.

He was still preparing answers to those questions when the door opened. As his captors snapped their feet together and gave the Nazi outstretched arm salute, Raffa studied the man standing in the doorway. He wore a German uniform.

"Dismissed. Our men will deal with Herr Wolff-Jaegar now," he told the sergeant.

"Heil Hitler," his escort shouted as they saluted yet again.

"Heil Hitler." Then the aide turned to Raffa and his emotionless face gave nothing away as he said, "This way, Herr Wolff-Jaegar. The major will see you now."

When he saw his interrogator, Raffa was glad that he'd worn his good suit even though it was now so scruffy. The major's black uniform looked as though it had been especially tailored for him. Two oak leaves on scarlet shoulder boards and collar patches proclaimed his German army rank and his white shirt was made from the finest Egyptian cotton. Raffa wondered if it had come from a Wolff-Jaegar mill. Just the thought of a Nazi in Wolff-Jaegar cotton made him queasy.

The major seemed curiously young for such a high position and he fiddled with some papers on his desk, almost as though he was indecisive about something. Finally he leaned back in his chair, made a steeple with his fingers, rocking back and forth as he studied Raffa.

When he spoke, his voice was quiet. "Herr Wolff-Jaegar, what were you doing on New Year's Eve in 1934?"

He's softening me up, Raffa thought as he stood at attention. It's 2 a.m. I'm tired, filthy and hungry. New Year's Eve? 1934? His brain was still preoccupied with thinking about ways to prevent Nazi control of the Wolff-Jaegar empire.

1934 seemed an eternity away but he knew it had sig-

nificance. His brain stalled and the wall clock's ticking sounded abnormally loud as he shook his head and tried to concentrate. Who remembered what they did four years earlier?

The major seemed to misunderstand his silence. Leaving his desk, he walked over to the fireplace and pointed to one of the armchairs near it. "Forgive me, Herr Wolff-Jaegar," he said. "Please sit here."

It's a trick, Raffa told himself, but he nevertheless welcomed the comfort of the fire and the armchair.

"New Year's Eve. 1934," the major repeated. "Please. What were you doing?"

Living another life in another universe, Raffa thought. Suddenly he remembered a glorious day of skiing and the night spent in a backbreaking search and rescue. He straightened and confidently faced the major.

"I spent New Year's Eve searching for an idiot skier lost in a blizzard on Garmisch-Partenkirchen. After I found him, I carried him down the mountain and then danced the last dance with the most beautiful woman I've ever met. My wife."

"I know," the major smiled. "Not about your wife's beauty, of course. I was referring to the rescue."

Good grief. Raffa felt the bottom drop out of his existence. If the Nazis had researched him so thoroughly, *keeping the Wolff-Jaegar businesses out of their hands seemed as impossible as parting the Red Sea. Yet, Moses had done the impossible. Maybe he could as well. He didn't say anything to the major. He just sat and waited for the interrogation to continue.*

To his surprise, the major smiled. "Herr Wolff-Jaegar. You are not understanding me at all. I was on the mountain that New Year's Eve."

Raffa remembered other groups of searchers but couldn't work out why the major kept talking about 1934. One part of him desperately wanted sleep; the other part pulsed with adrenaline and the need to stay alert. Sooner or later, the major's questions would become dangerous and Raffa couldn't afford to be caught half asleep.

Again, almost as though he was reading Raffa's mind, the major smiled. "I'm sorry, Herr Wolff-Jaegar. I would have introduced myself that night on the mountain—if I'd been conscious, that is. You see, I'm your idiot skier."

Raffa looked at the major, searching his face for some semblance to the snow-coated skier he'd saved. "I'm sorry, sir. I didn't recognize you."

The major waved his hand, dismissing the apology. "I knew I was going to die that night. My leg was broken. Then you came along. I don't remember much more than that because of the pain. I know you saved my leg by splinting it and I remember the song you sang as you struggled to make it down. You called me Bruno and talked to me. I still remember some of that conversation."

Oh no. Raffa vaguely remembered that he'd talked about Hitler's possible effect on Jews and what that meant to the Wolff-Jaegars.

"Bruno" commenced talking again. "You were gone by the time I came back from the hospital. I asked everywhere for you. When I could not find you, I swore I'd never forget the name of Raphael Wolff-Jaegar. You can imagine what I felt when I looked at the list of the internees today and your name was on the top."

Raffa studied the major again. Then, as now, he didn't know the man's name. He vaguely remembered calling him Bruno as they worked their way down the mountain. Tonight he saw a kindness lurking behind Bruno's army severity. Once again he wondered why he'd been brought to City Hall.

"A life for a life," the major said, abruptly breaking the silence. "That's what I'm offering you tonight."

Raffa sat forward. He understood. "What do I have to do?"

"Start with listening carefully," the major ordered, and this time there was absolutely no doubt about who was in charge. "I can only give you twenty-four hours. I'm being *transferred back to Berlin and my successor is expected here by then. Before I go, I'll make sure the prison records are in chaos and that you're not missed. Somebody is already working on that."*

Raffa started to say something but the major's hand went up. "Stop. No questions. The brownshirts," he broke off and grimaced as if they smelled like decaying fish. "They think you're being transferred to the camps. They're certain you can't escape because they confiscated every piece of your identification."

Raffa's heart and hope dropped. He shuddered at the thought of brownshirts pawing through his house. "My passport? I can't go anywhere without it."

Major Bruno allowed himself a small smile. "Your trip home will include a visit to Herr Braun's house. I understand he's the best forger in Vienna. For document purposes, you understand. Not art."

As the major paused, Raffa wondered exactly how much he knew and if the explanation about the forger was a tip-off that the Nazis had already identified Raffa's art dealer. Then he gave himself a shrug. Now wasn't the time to think about that. Now he had to listen carefully and make sure he understood everything.

As though he felt compelled to explain himself, Major "Bruno" cleared his throat and continued softly, "Herr

Wolff-Jaegar, my family has always served the Fatherland. We've never served a political party or its leader, so you understand this is dangerous for me. But I owe you my life. My aide? He owes you nothing and the only protection I can give him is anonymity. He will stay with you until Herr Braun brings your new travel documents. Then he will take you to the British Embassy. I understand you play tennis with the ambassador?"

Raffa knew right then that he and his family had seriously underestimated the Nazis. He might be one of the wealthiest men in world but did he justify this level of intelligence? He wanted to ask but knew he would get no answers. And while he might not get them, he was being given his life. What was more precious than that?

Almost as though he guessed what Raffa was thinking, Bruno allowed himself a slight smile. "Those tennis games, Herr Wolff-Jaegar, should help you get a visa for England. Make sure you tell the ambassador about your recent "conversion" to Anglicanism. Tell him to put Church of England instead of Jewish on your visa. Then, my friend, get on the first plane for London. My aide will stay until then. Do not suddenly decide to go anywhere for anything. We lost the entire Von Trapp family in Salsburg last night so everyone's twitchy. Capturing you might lessen the Fuhrer's anger."

The major stopped speaking and walked across to one of his cabinets. He poured whisky into two glasses and offered one to Raffa. After a sip, he stared at the fireplace before continuing, "My father is a member of the war ministry, Herr Wolff-Jaegar. I know the Fuhrer's plans. Do not put Jewish on any papers. Just get yourself far, far away from Europe. Don't stay in England. Go to Australia, or one of the other English colonies. This part of the world is going to be more dangerous than you can imagine, especially for your people."

While Raffa tried to absorb all he had heard, Bruno suddenly stood and clicked his heels together. He shouted, "To the Fatherland" and hurled his whisky glass into the fire.

At six o'clock the following night, Raffa sipped scotch in the luxury of the first class cabin on his flight to London.

Everything had gone exactly to the major's plan and Raffa realized he had been given a valuable lesson in the Nazi vision for Europe. After he picked up Ruthie and Thell, he would leave England and take what was left of his family far, far away.

He had never joked about Hitler and the Nazis. Unlike some of his friends who caricatured Hitler by comparing him to Charlie Chaplin, Raffa had feared for Austria's future. But the information Bruno had carefully revealed shook him to his core.

He had managed to get his Ruthie, Thell, and a portion of their assets out of Austria. He knew he was lucky. He'd had a miraculous escape and he still had some of his wealth.

But what about Adele and the men in Vienna's prisons? What would happen to them?

He knew what would happen to the poor, to anyone suspected of being different and, worst of all, Jewish. He took a fast gulp of scotch and said a prayer. They would have no chance at all with the Nazis. Earl Grey's pronouncement of "The lights going out all over Europe" was too poetic. A horrific plague was coming, and it would be worse than anyone had imagined.

15

When Jas finished, I understood the atmosphere in the classroom. Like everyone else, I needed more. Jas let her great-grandfather's story soak in for a moment or so and then she smiled.

None of us had ever seen Jas smile like that. Her smile was beyond happy, beyond exuberance. She was a Jaslyn Green that none of us could have dreamed of seeing. During the past week, she had gained a tremendous confidence and, it appeared, deep joy.

It showed as she said, "I promised proof. The best documentation I have is my great-grandfather's forged passport."

As the class gasped, the door at the back opened. We all turned as Mr. Dickson walked into the room. "This is Thell, the little boy I told you about at the beginning of the story," Jas said. "Thell is also Nathaniel Dickson of The Adele Trust and he's my grandfather."

Everyone was beyond shocked. There was silence while Mr. Dickson walked to the front. When he reached the front row, Kimberley Leung stood and began clapping. Immediately, like a tidal surge, the entire class did the same.

Mr. Dickson showed us Raffa's forged passport and his own, very legitimate, one. No wonder Raffa got out of Austria! They looked identical. Then he showed us other bits and pieces of other documents—a driver's licence from Detroit and identification from every city they stayed in until Vancouver. Raffa was never going to be caught without ID again. Then Mr. Dickson smiled and asked if we had any questions.

There was a shocked silence. Questions? Finally, Cathy Semple's hand went up. "Why is your name Dickson? Why not Wolff-Jaegar?"

A good question, one I'd wanted to ask. "Papa wanted to be Canadian," Mr. Dickson said. "As soon as we came to Vancouver, he bought the house that I still live in. I had two days to get settled and then Papa put me into school at the St. Nicholas School for Boys. When Sunday came, I went to Sunday School at the same church that Jas goes to. Every other day I went back there after school for English lessons with the rector. Papa's passport said Church of England and so I was brought up as an Anglican. That's why my side of the family is Anglican, not Jewish. The name change came a few months later. Papa took a nail and hammered it into a telephone book. It stopped at Dickson, a very Canadian name."

Tula George, Prim Heights' very own First Nations student, slowly put her hand up. "Mr. Dickson, do you remember what it was like when Hitler invaded?"

Mr. Dickson seemed lost in thought and when he answered he surprised everyone. "Yes, I'll never forget it. I thought a circus had come. There were bands in the streets, people laughed and cheered and I got cross with Mama because I wasn't allowed to go outside. Then, of course, Papa put us in the car and we drove off out of Austria. So my memories are mixed. I was happy, then angry and then terrified."

This was new. I'd never heard of Hitler's occupation of Vienna being compared with a circus. Now about ten more hands shot into the air as everyone wondered what else Mr. Dickson could tell us.

"What about your cousin Adele? Did she make it?" Myra Wang asked.

Mr. Dickson's face went sad. "No, she didn't. When I started my business in Vancouver, I kept a portion of the profits aside for her in a trust fund. I did that for seven long years until I found that she was one of the very first who died in the gas chambers. Even after that, I added her share. It was my way of keeping her memory alive. And then I thought of a different way to use Adele's trust fund and the rest is history."

Kimberley put her hand up and stood when Mr. Dickson acknowledged her. "Sir, I've read that a Montreal man in his nineties got his Klimt painting back. Did the art dealer manage to save your family's art?"

Mr. Dickson shrugged. "The Nazis offered the dealer one choice. His life or our art. They took everything. We have rescued about half of what we had, including the Cezanne." Mr. Dickson grinned as he looked around at us. "I've told Jas that she should enlist all her friends the next time she has a group project to see if you can track down more of it. There's a small Soutine that used to be in my bedroom in Vienna that I'd love to have back."

It must have seemed that all our heads were on a stick, because we simultaneously swivelled to look at Dr. Collins. "We'll see," she laughed. Then she thanked Mr. Dickson for coming in with the passports and congratulated him for having such a wise and courageous father.

The class swarmed around him, asking for autographs. When it was her turn, Patti Cheng asked, "Why is Jaslyn's name Green, not Dickson?"

The silence became absolute when Kimberley answered, "Don't be rude, Patti. That's not our business. It's private."

Like me, more than one girl looked at Kimberley and wondered who this new person was. I was still thinking about her as I waited for everyone to leave the room so that I could talk to Dr. Collins.

"I've worked hard," I told her. "But my presentation won't be like Jo's or Jas's. It's not dramatic or glamorous and I don't want them to suffer because of it. Can I be a group of one?"

Dr. Collins shook her head. "That wouldn't be fair, Jenn. I've made it clear from the beginning that it's a group mark. You're the 3Js not the 1J. But I think we all need a break. The class has had enough bombshells this week and I want to follow up on some things Mr. Dickson said. Take the weekend, Jenn, and give your report on Monday. Do your best. You might surprise yourself."

Not possible.

Jas and Jo tried to cheer me up on Saturday while we did each other's toenails. I shook my head at everything they said. Now that I had to talk about Great-great-grandfather, I couldn't sleep again. Researching him had changed me. I didn't have a happing ending. I really didn't have any ending at all so I knew my report would be like a million zits. Ugly. Ugly. Ugly.

Jo and Jas refused to listen when I told them I was going to drag the group mark down. "Think of it this way," Jas said. "Jo will score big-time. Probably, 100." She thought for a moment and then shrugged. "Nothing below 97, anyway. I think I'll get at least 90. Dr. Collins liked Grandfather and my written report is good. So even if you get a zero, Jenn, do the math. That's at least 187, so we'll average out to 60%. That's a C and it's a pass. Besides, I don't need straight As. I'm not a scholarship kid anymore."

Her smile was pure sunshine—except for the tiny bit of smug.

Jo stopped painting my nails and looked at me. "Dr. Collins tapes everything. Ask her for a copy and send it to your mom so that she doesn't pull Tahiti off the table. That's the worst case scenario because I think Jas is wrong. You'll get at least 50. Your written part is that good. That 50 plus the 187 is 237. If you divide that by three, it's a B for the group. Even if your oral part is as low as 18, we'll get an A. So, relax. Chill. Even if you blow the oral part, we'll be fine."

Once I thought about it, Jo was probably right. My research was solid, and I would get good marks for it. Plus, I felt comforted. I had friends and they had my back. I sort-of enjoyed the weekend.

That didn't stop me from getting the jitters when the time came for my presentation on Monday. Jo and Jas had pictures and music ready. My theme song was the 1931 hit, *As Time Goes By*.

I didn't dress in black. My story wasn't dramatic. When I walked to the front in my normal boarder's uniform, Great-great grandfather's face filled the smart board. He looked kind, benevolent. It went without saying that he was handsome. At Thanksgiving I'd thought that Cecil would look like him when he got older. Providing, of course, that he outgrew his obnoxiousness.

Because that was the thing about the sainted Henry. I don't think he was obnoxious. His views were but when he lived just about everyone else in Canada shared them.

I stood straight as I gave a synopsis of Great-great grandfather's life and achievements. Then I ended by saying: "Henry North guaranteed that Canada's soldiers and sailors had weapons and ships. He kept the mines running so that Canada's weapon quotas were met. For this, he truly deserved the awards and medals he got for service to his country. But there's more to his story than that. People are rarely black or white."

At this point Jo flashed the 1943 cartoon onto the smart board and I asked, "What do you think this means?"

After staring at Great-great grandfather's face for the last five minutes, everyone recognized him in the cartoon and started laughing.

"Something about sex with nuns?" Amelia Kristian asked.

The class laughed again but Dr. Collins looked intrigued. "That's what Jo said when I first showed it to her," I went on. "But it's really a political cartoon about Great-great grandfather's immigration policies. He believed that Canada needed farmers, loggers and miners and those were almost the only immigrants he allowed in."

"Then what's with the nuns?" Amelia asked and again the class laughed.

Jas sent a riff of Richard Wagner's *Ride of the Valkyries* throughout the room as Jo flashed photo after photo of Nazi storm troopers beating up German Jews and smashing shop windows on *Kristall-*

nacht. The final set of photos showed families wearing stars of David being herded into railroad cattle cars.

Someone muttered, "I hate World War II."

That broke the tension. When Jo put the nun cartoon back on the screen, I resumed talking.

"Last week, Mr. Dickson told us a little bit about what it was like if you were a Jew in Europe in the 1930s and everyone knows what happened to them during World War II. Yet my great-great grandfather made sure that Canada accepted very few refugees. His favourite saying was 'None is too many.' That's what the cartoon means."

"How many did we take?" Cathy Semple asked.

"About five thousand over ten years."

There was silence while everyone thought about that, and then Mary Grant asked, "Is that why Raffa made sure Mr. Dickson went to St. Nick's and your church?"

I nodded. "Obviously. And don't forget that Raffa came in on a visa that said he was Anglican, or Church of England as they called it back then. He also made sure he did everything right. He got something called an Order-in-Council to be here. I think that's how he bypassed Great-great grandfather."

"He was rich," Myra Wang commented.

I grinned at her. "And knew how to get what he wanted."

Cathy Semple put her hand up. "You said we took 5,000 Jewish people. But when did we take them? All at once, like after the war? And how does our record compare with other countries?"

This from the girl who never did any work? Was there a limit to surprises in Grade 9? If so, I'm sure we'd met it. It took a moment to work out how to answer her.

"First answer. I think Canada took those 5,000 Jews over a decade, roughly 1936-1946. The second answer's on the screen."

Jo put several graphs showing Jewish immigration to America, Australia, Brazil, Canada, and the United Kingdom onto the board. I pointed to one, "As you see, Canada's population was about eleven million. Australia had only seven million people yet it took more than five times more Jewish immigrants than we did."

Kimberley put her hand up, an extraordinary show of politeness. "The way I see it," she began and pointed to the graph in the centre. "When you look at immigrants per population, Australia took in one for every 250 of its citizens; the US admitted one Jew for every 830; and Canada one for every 2,200 people.

Why so few? Each country was vastly under-populated."

No wonder Kimberley got top marks in math. I hadn't looked at it from that way but I respected her sufficiently to believe that she'd got it right. I nodded to Jas who played "*As Time Goes By*" very softly.

"I don't think we can imagine what it was like to live during the 1940s. People were wired differently. I'll give two examples. The League of Nations, the 1930s version of the United Nations, called a conference in 1938 to talk about the Jewish refugees. Delegates had a great time. They golfed, took cruises on the lake near the city of Evian, and gambled at the casino. They also talked for ten days. When they finished, they said that Germany itself should solve the Jewish refugee problem. They called it a German domestic issue not an international one. I wonder if any of them lost sleep when they heard that Germany's "solution" meant a holocaust of more than six million people who didn't fit their ideas of perfection. All I know for sure is that judging from his diaries, my great-great grandfather didn't seem to regret his actions once the holocaust became general knowledge."

I paused for a moment and looked at the class, wondering if I had the guts to keep going. "When I first found out about Great-great-grandfather, I felt really ashamed of him. Really, really ashamed. I've thought a lot about him and realized that he thought he was doing the best thing. But his best thing meant that thousands and thousands of Jews couldn't come to Canada and they probably died in the death camps. I've fought with myself over him. I want to feel proud of him but I don't think I can and I've only just figured out why. It's because I see the Henry North of the 1940s through the eyes of Jennifer North of the 2010s."

Some of the class frowned and Kimberley looked like she wanted to ask a question. When I started talking again, I spoke slowly because I was still fumbling, still trying to make sense of my thoughts. "How many of you remember the movie *To Kill A Mockingbird*?"

Everyone snickered and Tula said, "Super-sub week."

Last year we'd had a substitute teacher for English who was really a gym teacher. He'd tried his best and that meant he rented videos of novels he'd seen in the book room. I grinned back at Tula when I continued, "Well, the author of that novel was a woman called Harper Lee. For fifty years everyone thought she was kind of perfect. She'd only written that one book and it won every possible literary award and just about every high school kid had to read it. Then a few years ago the impossible happened. Someone found the manuscript of a novel she'd written earlier than *Mockingbird*."

A couple of girls smiled like they already knew what I was talking about. When I asked my next question I didn't call on them to answer it. "What do you remember about Atticus Finch?"

Everyone smiled and words like "nice," "brave" and "gutsy" echoed around the room. Someone, it might have been Kimberley, whispered, "I wish he were my father."

That's why my next question hit so hard. "What would you say if I told you that he carried a Ku Klux Klan membership card in his pocket when he defended Tom Robinson?"

"I'd laugh and call you an idiot," Cathy Semple.

Jas played a little bit of *Rock Around the Clock* while Jo flashed the cover of *Go Set a Watchman* onto the smart board. "This novel by Harper Lee was published in 2015. It's so hard to realize that it's her first novel. Somehow it got lost for more than fifty years. In *Watchman* Harper Lee has the same characters. The strange thing is that they're older by about twenty years. It's also set in the 1950s, the same time that she wrote it. So Scout is in her twenties and Atticus, in his seventies, carries the KKK card in his wallet. Does this change your opinion of him?"

Dr. Collins had an expression of intense interest as she looked at me and then at the class. The silence must have stretched to two minutes before Patty said, "If he had it on him in his seventies, he must have also had it when he was fifty-whatever during the trial. He's a hypocrite, isn't he? I don't think I like him anymore."

Everyone started talking with each other and arguing. I didn't know how to stop them until Dr. Collins stood up. "It's a shock, isn't it? What do you think, Jenn?"

With that I knew I'd love Dr. Collins till I died. She had brought me back to my main point. "It's kind of like my great-great grandfather, isn't it? When Harper Lee grew up, her father probably had a KKK membership card as well. Most white men in the American South did back then. She wrote *Watchman* in the 1950s when protests against racism were just beginning. *Mockingbird* was published in the 1960s after the freedom marches had started and it became sort of fashionable to be against racism.

"I think if Great-great grandfather lived today and was running in an election for parliament, he'd condemn the holocaust and anyone who seemed to be anti-Semitic. He'd be like the rest of us and think it wrong. That's why this project has been so hard for me. I don't know what's right or wrong anymore. I've begun to question everything I believe in. I keep asking myself will I think differently about things in ten or twenty years. If so, which things? Is there anything I can believe in that won't change? I've thought about Great-great grandfather so many times. The only things he and I have in common seem to be that we love our families and go to church. I guess I appreciate my church because it hasn't changed much over the years."

"Well, not since Henry VIII," Kimberley said and I swear she was teasing me.

Everyone laughed.

"Like I said, I don't know the answers to my questions," I went on as Jas played the *As Time Goes By* music again. "I don't know what to think when things like tolerance change so radically between one generation and another. Science changes as well. Once they debated whether the earth was flat or round. They also believed that the sun revolved around the earth. Now, science has kind of replaced God and some people believe it's the only truth. Our behaviors change as dramatically and each generation seems scandalized by the next. Don't believe me? Think sex, we way we dress, and what our grand-mothers say."

I took a sip of water and looked at each of the girls in front of me and gulped a little as I continued, "Some secrets are so dangerous they should be forgot-ten. But others, like the murder of Jo's great-grand-father, need remembering. The bodies of Bill and his men weren't discovered in time to be included in the Nuremburg trials so no one was ever punished for that massacre. Canada has forgotten that little squad of Royal Winnipeg Rifles kneeling in a field as they waited to be gunned by teenagers barely old enough to shave. Somehow the squad's silent courage lacks the glamor of D-Day. Yet, they also endured landing on Juno beach."

"I'll remember Bill next Remembrance Day," Cathy Semple volunteered.

I smiled. Cathy volunteering to do something? Yet, I knew she was serious and that she would think about Bill on November 11. "My great-great grand-father's Jewish policies have been forgotten because, nowadays, it's so convenient to forget how recently we were so racist."

"Recently? It's over sixty years ago," Patti inter-jected.

"Well, recent in terms of history and at that time Vancouver was pretty racist, much like the rest of Canada. We didn't allow Chinese or Japanese swimmers in English Beach then and Tula will probably know that First Nations people weren't allowed to vote until the 1960s. I think present-day Canada shows that a lot of racism can be eliminated. Of course, it won't ever be totally gone. But today so many groups of people in Vancouver get along fine. Maybe Canadians are different from most other countries. America was founded on "Life, Liberty, and the Pursuit of Happiness." Our much less glamorous idea was "Peace, Order, and Good Government." That's what Great-great-grandfather North believed in and it's still the basis for what we want as Canadians."

I took another sip of water as I looked around the class again. I'd known many since kindergarten. Others were new friends, like Jas and Jo. Some, like Cathy and Kimberley, I now realized, I might not know at all.

"History's judgment on Henry North far outweighs the popularity he had when he was alive. I've thought hard about my beliefs and what they are based on. I don't know what my sins of omission are, but I do know that I don't want my great-great granddaughter to research me and feel bitterly ashamed. And that's the challenge. Do we all go along with things, following the crowd? Are we for racism in one generation, against it the next? Do we ever wonder if what we do is ultimately right or wrong? I never thought about things like that until I studied Great-great grandfather."

There was silence until Tula put her hand up. "It's true that I, as a First Nations, wouldn't have been allowed to vote back then. One of my grandmothers still has the card she got allowing her to vote in the 1960s." She looked around and grinned cheekily, "I don't think I would have been allowed to come to school here either, would I?"

I'd seen some Primrose Heights class photos from the 1940s. The faces were pure white. Happy faces but, nonetheless, pure white. As I fumbled for a response, the bell rang and rescued me.

16

On the second Saturday in December, Jo, Jas and I sat on my bed doing our favorite Saturday morning thing. Toenails. The big Dickson party was later that night and we wanted to look perfect.

Simone had sent a new dress for the occasion.

Yes, via Grandmother, who was happily ensconced at the Dicksons. She'd stay there for another week. Then she'd meet Mandy at the airport and take the twenty minute flight across to Qualicum. That is, providing the weather was good. If not, she'd have to do the five hour ferry thing like the rest of us.

I could hear Mom singing away in the kitchen and it felt wonderful. She had flown in yesterday and was home for good. Judging from the pieces of luggage, she'd brought back every single thing she'd taken east. Obviously the differences between Dad and her were irreconcilable.

It still hurt but not as much as it had at first. When I was a little older, I'd make Dad have time for me. I missed him but not like I had in September. Time, apparently, does heal.

Mom would have to find another housekeeper. Mrs. Green was moving out. There'd almost been an earthquake, what with the Green plate pushing against the Dickson one. The Dicksons had offered Mrs. Green a suite in their mansion. Mrs. Green said no. She thought a condo might be acceptable. It had gone on and on until someone brokered a deal.

Ordinarily the Dicksons would have been in Hawaii at their family compound but finding Jas had kept them here in Vancouver. They'd fly down next week and Jas and her mom would go with them. When Jas and Mrs. Green came back, they'd move into the Dicksons' house on a temporary basis. If Mrs. Green decided she didn't want to live there, she'd have plenty of time to find something else.

If she did, Jas's trust fund would pay for it.

Things were changing for Jo, as well. Mr. Carruthers had arrived the previous weekend and begun looking at houses. Jo wanted to stay at Leith as a boarder so she thought he should look for a condo instead of a house. Compared with the Green-Dickson debate their argument was nothing. Nevertheless I hated seeing it because I knew Mom and I would be having much the same discussion. Like Jo, I wanted to stay at Leith. It was my comfort blankie at the moment.

I had even given my commitment to play tennis for the rest of the year. For one thing I'd started to enjoy it and, as Mr. Carruthers had told us in Toronto, Jo and I had something magical. We somehow knew what each other was going to do and that was like having a third player on the court.

While I zoned, I was vaguely aware of Jas and Jo talking about Christmas. Now, I realized that talk had escalated into another argument. I knew why, of course.

Jas had turned into a trust fund trainwreck.

Sometime during the past week, she had found out that Mr. Dickson owned his own plane. Since then she'd begun a campaign to get all of us down to Hawaii for at least a week, even Mike.

Jo looked at me. "Tell her, once more, that you're spending Christmas at QBeach. That's what your grandmother came out here for and what Mandy's expecting."

Jas made a noise that sounded like bosh. "Jenn's

grandmother's already agreed to come and I bet Mandy would take Hawaii over Qualicum any day."

Like I said, a mini-trainwreck. She wasn't doing drugs or anything like that but she was becoming addicted to showering Mr. Dickson's money over everyone she knew. Her Christmas presents to the class had been so extravagant that Dr. Collins had phoned both Mom and Mr. Dickson for advice as to whether or not we could keep them.

I reckoned Mrs. Green and Mr. Dickson would give Jas another week or so and then rein her back to reality. I sure hoped so.

Suddenly, our phones pinged. Dr. Collins had finally sent our marks. When I saw mine, I sighed with relief. I hadn't cost Jas and Jo. I wasn't sure if Dr. C was an easy marker or if everyone had done exceptionally well because she'd handed out As like Mrs. Robinson used to do. Half the class had one and we'd tied with Kimberley's group at the top with 99.

Strangely enough, I didn't resent that. I was coming to respect Kimberley. Maybe, we'd even become friends.

Her written presentation had been exquisite. As promised. Mrs. Leung had to feel that she'd received her money's worth. When Kimberley had started her oral presentation, she thanked me for giving her the courage to talk honestly about her feelings. She described herself a "birth refugee," explaining that her father had began making arrangements to get her mother and her out of China as soon as she was born.

He'd wanted a son that badly.

He now lived back in Beijing with an alternate family. Although Mrs. Leung finally produced the longed-for boy, Kimberley only saw her father twice a year when she flew over to see him. She explained what it felt like to come second to Chinese expectations and how she was expected to be Chinese when, in fact, she knew she couldn't function there. She was determined to stay in Canada. She valued our democracy and wanted to bring her future children up here.

So I couldn't resent having the same mark as her. We'd done much the same journey. But our English mark sealed the deal for Tahiti. I had met Mom's criteria. That's why I felt so conflicted over Jas's determination to fly us all down to Hawaii for ten days or so. Warm ocean water had been a powerful motivation during the term because of my struggle with Henry North and trying to work out Dad. The thought of Tahiti had helped me grind out tennis training. Would going to Hawaii lessen the dream of relaxing in Bora-Bora over an extended spring break?

Our phones pinged again. It was Mom. "Downstairs. Now," she'd messaged.

Our dates for the party had arrived. Not properly dressed, of course, but our collective parents wanted to make sure that everyone knew what was what. I don't know if "dates" was the right word. It was for Jas and Jo. As Blake's parents had been invited, he'd asked me to go with him. I won't be fifteen till Christmas so Mom's still hyper-queasy about me calling anything, except coffee, a date.

Talking about queasy, Axel, Caleb and Blake looked like they might be sick at any moment. Mike came up from the basement and all four males sat on the edge of their chairs, their backs as straight as soldiers on parade.

Mom started the ball rolling, "The one thing that's essential about tonight is that you realise this is one of the Dicksons' proudest moments. It's the presentation of a long lost daughter-in-law and granddaughter. You must understand that Jas will be stared at for the entire evening. Do you get that?"

"Yes," the guys said, almost with one voice. I nodded, feeling sorry for Jas. She put her head down and Jo squeezed her hand.

"Axel," Mr. Carruthers said. "You're going to have to man up and take the pressure. Shield Jas as much as you can. Get her away from uncomfortable situations. Caleb and Blake will help you. So will we. Understand?"

As though they were synchronized, the guys nodded.

"I can be a bodyguard," Mike offered. He was staying over to go to the party and had even consented to rent a tux. He'd rolled his eyes and grumbled of course but I knew how proud and happy he was to be thought of as family.

Mr. Carruthers hadn't finished. "One of the sad facts about growing up," he began, "is that you find people with very different senses of right and wrong. Sometimes people think it's funny to put drugs into drinks. All of you watch for that, even you, young Mike. There'll be a couple of hundred people there. If you put your glass down get a new one when you want to drink again even if you've only taken one sip. Got it?"

"One more thing about drinks," Mrs. Green added. "There'll be champagne toasts. We're allowing you one sip each time it happens. No more. And don't forget, you'll be on show. Don't slip up."

"I know Jenn won't," Mom said and then added the five words that always struck terror into me, "Her grandmother will be watching."

Everyone laughed and the adults went back to the kitchen. The rest of us got our coats and scarves and headed outdoors to Starbucks. "I remember watching Prince William and Kate's wedding," Caleb said on the way. "This thing tonight sounds exactly like it."

We laughed at his hyperbole but I knew what he meant. I turned to Jas, "How are you coping?"

"I keep thinking it's like the tennis dance. I was sort of on show there and I had a wonderful time. I don't think I'll get into any trouble and, if I do, I have all of you, our parents, Jenn's grandmother and my own grandparents watching out for me. That's enough security for anyone."

I decided right then and there that I wanted to hug a dolphin on my fifteenth birthday. That is, if they had dolphins in Hawaii. I didn't care if Jas asked the guys, Jo's dad and Mr. French either. As she'd just said, there would be enough security for everyone.

It had been a tough term for all of us. Suddenly blue skies, warm water and sand sounded appealing. As soon as school resumed, Jo and I would be pounding tennis balls for real. I'd got a floater's gift with my math mark and I needed to bring it up a little more. Not that I wanted to, but getting straight As was part of my deal with Mom.

Besides, it would make looking forward to Tahiti that much better.

TRUE OR FALSE?

The three historical stories in the book are constructed from fact.

Some of you will have seen the movie *Woman in Gold* in which Helen Mirren plays Maria Altman. Maria fought the Austrian government and a Vienna museum for ownership of a portrait of Adele Bloch-Bauer painted by Gustav Klimt. The Raffa story is connected in that it tells the true story of one of Adele's relatives, Leopold (Poldi) Bloch-Bauer, and his escape from Austria on a forged passport with Church of England visa. Poldi brought his family to Vancouver, changed Bloch-Bauer to Bentley and was instrumental in founding one of the nation's giant timber companies—Canadian Forest Products.

Jaslyn's story of the Dickson family and its secrets

are completely fictional and have *zero* connection with the Bentleys.

William Stewart Ferguson of Vancouver joined the Royal Winnipeg Rifles in 1940. He and more than forty other soldiers were massacred by the HitlerJu-gend, on 8 June 1944, two days after D-Day while prisoners of war. This heinous war crime went unpunished and is still largely forgotten. Nobody knows why he demoted himself to lieutenant. His official records states over and over that the demotion was by his own request and I believe, as I wrote in the book, that he demoted himself to join his men on D-Day.

Jenn's great-great-grandfather is based on the actions and words of two cabinet ministers. Their immigration policies may be found in Irving M. Abella and Harold M. Troper's book, *None is Too Many.*

Without the help of Lesley Bentley who told me about Poldi, her grandfather-in-law, this book would never have happened. My late husband, F. Murray Greenwood, first interested me in Bill Ferguson's fate and Chris Greenwood filled in some gaps of his grandfather's fifty-four hour war and encouraged me to write about it. Patricia Kennedy of Archives Canada generously helped me try to unknot several problem in Bill Ferguson's military record. Nobody, though, could definitively solve the mystery of the initials L.O.

While the stories of Henry North, Raffa and Bill are imagined to fit the broad base of facts, I am responsible for any gross misrepresentations and/or errors.

ACKNOWLEDGEMENTS

I'm grateful to everyone who helped with this book and its previous incarnation as *The 3Js*. My then writers' group (Melanie Anastasiou, Paul O'Rourke, Susan Pieters, Kathy Tyers, Gordon Wilson) patiently critiqued various drafts; members of the Bentley family–Michael, Spencer and Lesley, in particular–greatly encouraged me; and Bronwyn Short commented on various drafts. Thanks as well to Jane Kuizinas and Wayne Gatley for their insights and help with the revised work. I appreciate the hours of work you've given me.

As he has done for all my books, Chris Greenwood examined the text with his eagle eye. The remaining errors are mine.

This is the hardest book I've written and even now I wonder if I have it right because it doesn't build to the traditional climax. Rather it deals with shame caused by an ancestor's beliefs and the uncertainty they cause in the protagonist's life. *Forgotten Secrets* asks us to think about ourselves, our underlying beliefs and what they are based on and to endeavour to live so that our descendants won't feel the need to apologize for our behaviours.

ABOUT THE AUTHOR

Beverley Boissery was born in Sydney, Australia and lives in Vancouver with her now very aged feline friend, Lillee. Her books have won many awards, the Surrey Invitational Writers Conference Special Achievement Award and she was a grateful recipient of a Canada Council grant. She enjoys hearing from her readers Please email her at boissery@shaw.ca or try through her erratic website — boissery.com.

Published by The Dundurn Group

THE SOPHIE MALLORY (REBELLIONS OF 1837 SERIES)

Sophie's Rebellion

Sophie's Treason

Sophie's Exile

Published by Wesbrook Bay Books

THE WAHMURRA SERIES

The Convict's Thumbprint

tHAD

THE THEO BENTLEY GOES TO WAR SERIES

Theo Bentley's War of 1812

PRIMROSE HEIGHTS SCHOOL SERIES

Forgotten Secrets

CPSIA information can be obtained
at www.ICGtesting.com
Printed in the USA
BVHW042320141118
533144BV00006B/28/P